PRAISE FOR

Me and My Baby View the Eclipse

"Sparkles like diamonds . . . 'Tongues of Fire' is, quite simply, one of the best short stories I've ever read."

—*Chicago Tribune*

"Smith is at her best. . . . Peepholes of insight light up the best stories. Before we can blink, we're dazzled."

—*USA Today*

"Revelatory writing from a master storyteller . . . Tiny explosions, little surprises, minor epiphanies pepper the lives of Smith's characters in her latest collection."

—*Library Journal*

"Smith's insights and the graceful, effortless prose place her characters firmly in their regional—yet universal—milieu."

—*Publishers Weekly*

"Rings so true you wonder if she doesn't know your own mother." —*Greensboro Daily News & Record*

"If you like her novels, you'll love her short stories."

—*The Charlotte Observer*

Me and My Baby
View the Eclipse

LEE SMITH

BERKLEY BOOKS, NEW YORK

THE BERKLEY PUBLISHING GROUP
Published by the Penguin Group
Penguin Group (USA) LLC
375 Hudson Street, New York, New York 10014

USA • Canada • UK • Ireland • Australia • New Zealand • India • South Africa • China

penguin.com

A Penguin Random House Company

Berkley trade paperback ISBN: 978-0-425-27186-5

The Library of Congress has cataloged the G. P. Putnam's Sons hardcover edition as follows:

Smith, Lee, date.
Me and my baby view the eclipse : stories / by Lee Smith.
p. cm.
Contents: Bob, a dog—Mom—Life on the moon—Tongues of fire
—Dreamers—The interpretation of dreams—Desire on Domino Island
—Intensive care—Me and my baby view the eclipse.
ISBN 0-399-13507-3
I. Title.
PS3569.M5376M4   1989   89-27377 CIP
813'.54—dc20

PUBLISHING HISTORY
G. P. Putnam's Sons hardcover edition / 1990
Ballantine Books mass-market edition / February 1991
Ballantine Books trade paperback edition / July 1997
Berkley trade paperback edition / December 2014

PRINTED IN THE UNITED STATES OF AMERICA

10 9 8 7 6 5 4 3 2 1

Cover art: Church Spire in Small Town © Joe Sohm / Getty Images.
Cover design by Royce M. Becker.
Interior text design by Laura K. Corless.

Four of the stories in this volume, some in slightly different form, first appeared in the
following magazines, to whose editors grateful acknowledgments is made: "Life on
the Moon" (as "Good-bye, Sweetheart") and "Me and My Baby View the Eclipse"
in *Redbook*; "The Interpretation of Dreams" in *Southern Magazine*; and "Intensive Care"
in *Special Report: Fiction*. "Bob, a Dog" was published in a limited edition by
Mud Puppy Press, Chapel Hill, North Carolina, in 1988.

The author gratefully acknowledges permission to reprint lyrics from "Heartbreak Hotel"
by Mae Boren Axton, Tommy Durden, and Elvis Presley, at page 74.
Copyright © 1955 Tree Publishing Co., Inc. Copyright renewed. All rights reserved.
International copyright secured. Used by permission of the publisher.

For Faith Sale

CONTENTS

Bob, a Dog

It was early May, two days after his thirty-ninth birthday, when David left her forever. "Forever"—that's what he said. He stood in the downstairs hallway turning an old brown hat around and around in his hands. Cheryl had never seen the hat before. She stood on the stairs above him, coming down, carrying towels. David said he needed a different life. Behind him, the door was wide open. It was sunny and windy outside. She had made him a carrot cake for his birthday, she was thinking—now what would she do with the rest? Nobody liked carrot cake except David and Angela, who was dieting. Angela was always dieting. David continued to talk in his calm, clipped way, but it was hard to hear what he said. He sounded like background noise, like somebody on the TV that Cheryl's mother kept going all the time in the TV room now since she had retired from her job at the liquor store. David wore cutoff jeans and an old plaid shirt he'd had ever since she'd met him, nearly twenty years before. She must have washed that shirt a hundred times. Two hundred times. His knees were thin and square. He was losing his hair. At his back, the yard was a blaze of sun.

Cheryl could remember the first time she ever saw him like it was yesterday, David standing so stiff and straight in the next-to-back pew of the Methodist church, wearing a navy-blue suit, and everybody whispering about him and wondering who he was, him so prim and neat it never occurred to any of them he might be from the Peace Corps, which he was. He didn't look like a northern hippie at all. He was real neat. Cheryl and her sister, Lisa, and her brother, Tom, were sitting right behind him, and after a while of looking at the careful part in his hair and his shoulder blades like wings beneath his navy suit, Cheryl leaned forward and gave him her program so he would know what was going on. He acted like somebody who had never been in a church before, which turned out to be almost true, while Cheryl's own family was there of course every time they cracked the door.

But oh, it seemed like yesterday! He was dignified. And he sat so straight. He might have been a statue in a navy-blue suit, a figurine like all those in Mamaw's collection. Cheryl had sucked in her breath and bitten her lip and thought, before she fell head over heels in love right then, that she ought to be careful. Because she had always been the kind of big, bouncy girl who jumps right in and breaks things without ever meaning to, a generous, sweet, well-meaning girl who was the apple of everybody's eye.

Cheryl handed him the program, and touched his hand too long. After the recessional she took him into the fellowship hall for a cup of Kool-Aid and wrote her telephone number down on a paper napkin before he even asked for it. "He's just my type," she said to her mother, Netta, later. "Ha!" Netta said. Netta thought he looked nervous. But Cheryl liked that about him, because everybody else she knew was exactly like their parents were, exactly like everyone else. David was older, a college graduate. Cheryl, who had finished high school two years before, was working then at Fabric World. She thought David was like a young man in a book, or a movie. Whatever he said seemed important, as if it had been written down and he was reading it aloud.

Later, when she got to know him, she'd go to the room that he rented over Mrs. Bailey's garage and lie with him on the mattress on the floor, where he slept—the mattress pulled over to the window where you could look right out on Thompson's Esso and the back road and the river winding by—and sometimes afterward she'd open her eyes to find him looking out this window, over the river, and she couldn't tell what he was thinking. She never knew what he thought. Then, Cheryl found this romantic.

But probably she should have gotten herself a big old man who could stand up to things, not that she didn't have offers. Look at Jerry Jarvis, who had always loved her, or Kenny Purdue, who she was dating at the time. When she told Kenny she didn't want to go out with him anymore because she was in love with David Stone from Baltimore, Maryland, Kenny went out and cried and rolled in the snow. That's what his mother told Netta on the telephone: she said Kenny rolled in the snow. But David Stone had a kind of reserve about him, a sort of hollow in him, which just drove Cheryl wild. It was like she was always trying to make up to him for something, to make something be okay, or go away, but she never knew what it was.

David came from a small quiet family, one sister and a shy divorced mother with her hair in a little gray bun on the top of her head, and a father who was not mentioned. At the time she met David, Cheryl didn't know anybody who was divorced. Now everybody was. Including her, it looked like. With David leaving forever, Cheryl would be divorced too. Should she put up her hair in a bun? Cheryl would be a divorcée. Like her sister, Lisa, like her best friend, Marie, like everyone on television.

This seemed totally crazy with all the towels she held in her arms, with how fresh and sweet they smelled. With the bedrooms upstairs behind her so full of all the children, of their shared life. Now Netta would say, "I told you so."

She'd swear up and down that she wasn't a bit surprised. And even Cheryl knew—had known when she married him—that David wasn't exactly a family man. She'd had four children knowing it, thinking that he would change. Because she loved him, and love conquers all. You can't decide who you're going to love.

And even though David didn't really believe in God and made fun of their cousin Purcell, an evangelist, and taught at the community college all these years instead of getting a real job, and refused to help Louis make a car out of wood that time for the Pinewood Derby in Cub Scouts, even so, there were other things—good things—as well. He liked to cook, he read books to her out loud, he'd been the one who got up with the babies in the night. It was weird to find these traits in a man, although they were more common now since women's lib than they had been when David and Cheryl got married, all those years ago.

Cheryl looked down the stairs at David, memorizing him.

"Please don't blame yourself," he said formally. "I feel terrible about doing this."

"Oh, that's okay," Cheryl said without thinking, because she had gone for so long pleasing men.

David started to say something else, and didn't. He turned sharp on his heel like a soldier and plunged out into the shiny day, right through Louis and his friends playing catch in the yard, and got in the Toyota and drove away. Cheryl stood in the doorway and watched him go and couldn't imagine a different life. She wondered if David would wear the hat.

Netta did not say "I told you so." Instead she cried and cried, sitting in her pink robe on the sofa in the TV room surrounded by blue clouds of Tareyton smoke. You would have thought that David Stone had left *her*, instead of her daughter Cheryl. But Netta, now sixty-two, had always been a dramatic woman. When her own husband, Cheryl's father, Bill, died suddenly of a heart attack at forty-nine, Netta had almost died too. She referred to that time now as "when Bill was tragically taken from us," but the truth was, it *was* tragic. Cheryl's father had been a kindly, jovial man, a hard worker.

Not like David Stone, who was, as Cheryl's friend Marie put it, an enigma. Marie came over a lot after David left, to help Cheryl cope. Marie was divorced too. She went to group therapy. "He was just an enigma," she said. That seemed to settle it as far as Marie was concerned, only of course it didn't.

For one thing, although David had left forever, he didn't go very far, just about four miles out the Greensboro highway, where he rented an apartment in the Swiss Chalet Apartments, which looked like a row of gingerbread houses. At first the kids liked going over there, especially because of the pool, but then they didn't because their daddy wouldn't get a TV or buy soft drinks or meat. According to Angela, he said he was going to simplify his life.

"Isn't it a little bit *late* for that?" Lisa asked when she heard this news. Lisa, who ran the La Coiffure salon in the mall, had had one so-so marriage and one big disaster, and always took a dim view of men anyway. She disagreed with Marie and felt that David was an asshole instead of an enigma.

Cheryl sat among these women—Lisa, Marie, and Netta—in her own velvet armchair in her own TV room, feeling like she wasn't even there. What Angela said about David simplifying his life reminded Cheryl of the old days, the really old days, when she lay with him on that mattress pulled over to the window in the room over Mrs. Bailey's garage, when the sun fell through the uncurtained windows in long yellow blocks of light, warming their bodies. She remembered the way the leaves looked, yellow and red and gold, floating on the river that October. David had loved her so much then. Whatever weird stuff he might be saying or doing now, David had loved her then.

"Good riddance, I say," said Netta, lighting up. David had made no bones about how much he hated cigarettes. If they hadn't been living in Netta's own house, he'd have made her go out in the yard to smoke.

"It might just be the male menopause," Marie offered. Marie was thin and pretty, with long pale legs and a brand-new perm which Lisa had just given her. Marie and Cheryl had been best friends since grade school. "He might turn right around and try to come back," said Marie.

"Ha!" said Netta. "Never!"

But Cheryl seized on this, thinking, *He might come back.*

Marie's other insight, seconded by their cousin Purcell, was that David's sister's dying of cancer so recently had a lot to do with this whole thing. Louise had died that January, before he left. She was forty-seven, a sweet shadowy English teacher who had never married. She was so shy. Yet it was surprising how many people had showed up at her funeral: ex-students, friends, people from their neighborhood in Baltimore. Cheryl, who never could find much to say to Louise, had been amazed. Louise had lived with David's mother, and now David's mother lived alone. David used to call them up every Sunday night. Now he probably called his mother. Cheryl bit her lip. David leaving was like him dying, was exactly like a death.

The first week, for instance, everybody in the neighborhood brought food. Mrs. Tindall brought her famous homemade vegetable soup, and Mr. and Mrs. Wright, across the street, sent a twenty-six-dollar platter of cold cuts from the Piggly Wiggly, where he was the manager. Helen Brown brought chicken and biscuits, Margaret Curry brought enough chili to feed a crowd. Other people brought other things. Then Johnnie Sue Elderberry came in bringing a carrot cake and Cheryl sat right down on the floor and burst into tears.

"Mama, *get up*," Angela said. Since her daddy left, Angela had gone off her diet and started smoking, and nobody had the heart to tell her to quit. Angela was sixteen.

"Sometimes God provides us with these hidden opportunities for growth and change," remarked Mr. Dodson Black, their minister. But Purcell, their cousin the evangelist, disagreed. "I'd like to get ahold of him," Purcell said. "I'd like to wring his neck." Purcell was a big blond man with a bright green tie. Lisa and Marie were putting all the extra food they couldn't eat right then into white plastic containers and freezing it. They put labels on the tops of the containers. Finally Cheryl got up from the floor. "Don't make any big decisions for the first year," warned their cousin Inez Pate, who had come on the bus from Raleigh to see how they were holding up. "Try some of this meatloaf," said Marie. "You've got to keep up your strength."

But Cheryl couldn't eat a thing. She was losing weight fast. She was wearing some nice gray pants that hadn't fit her for the last two years. She pushed the meatloaf away and said something to Marie and something to Purcell and went out the back door, under the porch light, which wasn't working because Louis had shot it out with his BB gun. He was shooting everything these days. Cheryl couldn't keep up with him. "It's *okay*. He's expressing his *anger*," Marie had said. But Cheryl wouldn't have a light fixture or a breakable thing left in the whole house, at this rate.

She sighed and wiped her forehead. It was hot. Every summer, her whole family had rented the same house at Morehead City for two weeks. This year what would they do? What would they ever do? It was almost dark. Shadows crept up from the base of the trees, from the hedge, from the snowball bush, from the nandina alongside the house. Cheryl had grown up in this very house, she'd played in this backyard. Her daddy used to bring packing boxes home from the store and help her cut windows and doors in them for playhouses.

Cheryl walked out in the yard and stood by the clothesline, looking back at the house which was black now against the paling sky, all its windows lighted, for all the world like one of those packing-box playhouses which she hadn't thought about in years. It was *her* family, *her* house, she had opened all these doors and windows for David, had given it all to him like a present. It was crazy that he had left. *He'll come back*, she thought.

But in the meantime she was going to have to go back to work, because even though David had simplified his life so much and even though Netta had a pension and they got some money all along from the rent of Daddy's coal land, anyway, things were getting tight all around. Luckily Johnnie Sue was pregnant again, so Cheryl could fill in for her over at Fabric World while she thought about her options. One thing she was considering was starting up her own slipcover business. Slipcovers had come back in style, slipcovers were big now. Cheryl wished her mother would go out and get a job too. Her mother was driving Angela crazy. "Don't make any big decisions," said Inez Pate. Poor Inez was aging so fast, she put a blue rinse on her hair now, it looked just awful. Cheryl held on to the clothesline and wept. But she didn't have to make any real big decisions, because of course he'd come back. It was just the male menopause, he'd come back. How could a man leave so many children?

And Cheryl thought of them now, of Angela too grown-up for her age, too big-breasted and smart-mouthed, smoking, suddenly too much like Lisa; of Louis, who'd always been edgy, getting in fights at school; of Mary Duke, only six, and whiny, who didn't really understand; and of Sandy, who was most like his father, so sober and quiet his nickname had always been too sporty for him.

Right after David left, Sandy had run away for four or five hours, and when Purcell finally found him down by the river he said he was sorry he was so bad, he knew his daddy had left because he was so bad. Purcell had brought him home in the rain coughing, and Sandy was still coughing, although Dr. Banks couldn't find any reason for it. Dr. Banks said the cough was just nerves.

Suddenly Cheryl heard a funny, scraping noise. And speaking of Sandy, here he came up the driveway, dragging a box along the gravel, walking backward, coming slow.

"Mama?" he said.

Then suddenly Cheryl felt like she hadn't actually seen Sandy, or any of her other children, for years and years, even though they had been right here. She had been too wrought up to pay them any mind. "What are you doing, honey?" she said.

Sandy pulled the box more easily across the grass and stopped when he reached her. "Lookie here," he said, leaning over, reaching down. Netta opened the back door just then and hollered, "Cheryl?" Cheryl looked down in the darkness, down in the box. Sandy coughed. His hair caught the light for a minute, a blur of gold. Netta slammed the door. Sandy straightened up with something in his arms that made a snuffling, slurping noise.

"Mama, this is Bob," he said.

There's been something wrong with that dog from the word go," Netta said later. "You never should have said yes in the first place. Yes was always your big mistake."

But by then, by the time Netta got around to "I told you so," it was way too late. Sandy just loved Bob to death. The first thing Sandy did after school every day was throw down his books on the hall floor and run into the TV room to see how Bob was doing. Every day Bob was doing the same. He lay between the sofa and the wall, hiding. When he heard Sandy coming, he thumped his tail. But he refused to stay outside. When they put him outside, he sank against the wall of the house and wailed, the longest wail, the most pitiful thing you ever heard. He sounded like Cheryl felt.

The kids thought that this was because he had been abused, and abandoned—Sandy had found him in the weeds along the interstate, near the overpass. Lisa said Bob wouldn't go out because he was stupid. She said he'd never learn anything and said they should take him straight to the pound before they got too attached to him.

But by then it was clear that the kids, especially Sandy, were already too attached.

And if they took Bob to the pound, he'd never find another home. People want a watchdog, a hunting dog. Nobody wants a dog that won't even go outside. Especially not one of this size. Because Bob was growing. It was clear he was getting big. Everybody had an opinion about what kind of dog he was, and although nobody knew for sure, Purcell felt certain he was at least half hound. He had that pretty red freckling, those long ears, and that kind of head. But he hung his head and walked sideways, getting behind the couch. He put his tail down between his legs. Bob looked ashamed, like he didn't have any pride. And the TV room smelled awful, as Netta pointed out.

"It's him or me," she said.

"It's him, then," said Angela, who was tired of having her grandmother at home all the time.

But then Lisa offered Netta a job at La Coiffure, making appointments and keeping the books, so she was gone nine to five anyway. Bob had the TV room to himself. He used a newspaper, but he wouldn't go outside. As he got older, his messes got bigger. This was supposed to be the children's job, cleaning up after Bob, but before long Cheryl noticed she was doing it all by herself. She did it in the mornings before she left and again when she came back home from Fabric World. She sprayed the den with Pine-Sol all the time. She got a stakeout chain so the kids could put Bob out in the yard in the afternoon, so they could get in the den to watch TV. It was clear then that Purcell was right, that Bob had some hound in him for sure, because of the way he howled.

The neighbors, who had been nice about Louis's shooting out all the streetlights and nice about Angela's new boyfriend's motorcycle, complained.

"He'll get used to it," Cheryl told them. "He'll quit."

But she didn't believe it either. One problem was that Bob was so dumb he kept tangling himself in his stakeout chain. He'd tangle his chain around the lawn chair, or the barbecue grill, or the snowball bush.

"I guess I need to build him a pen," Cheryl said.

"I think you need to get rid of him," said Marie.

"Well . . ." Cheryl said in that slow, thinking way she had. She stared off into the purple dusk beyond the backyard, beyond Bob on his chain and Marie in a lawn chair, drinking a gin and tonic. Somehow it had gotten to be June. Now Marie was having dates with Len Fogle, a local Realtor. She came by every day after work for a gin and tonic and described these dates in detail: where they went, what she wore. When Cheryl sat back in the lawn chair and closed her eyes, listening, it was almost like *she* was the one on the date, and she could imagine herself back with David again. "Then he kissed me in the car," Marie said. "He's got this little Honda? Then he asked if he could come up for a nightcap and I said yes." *Nightcap* was a dating word, a word Cheryl hadn't heard for years and years. She imagined herself and David having a nightcap in Marie's apartment, she imagined David putting his hand on her knee. "I was so glad I'd changed the sheets," said Marie. Cheryl sighed.

The real David was dating somebody else, a frizzy-headed math teacher at the community college who didn't even wear any makeup or shave her legs. Her name was Margaret Fine-Manning. She had been married before. But she was young. Last weekend her yellow Datsun had been parked at David's Swiss Chalet apartment from eleven in the morning until nine or ten that night; Cheryl just happened to know this because she had formed the habit of driving past the Swiss Chalets on her way to work, and then maybe if she ran out to the highway to pick up a burger or what she usually got, a fish sandwich, on her lunch hour, and then maybe also on her way home.

David was growing a beard. He looked skinny and picturesque, like a scientist in a documentary, like Jacques Cousteau. He was getting a tan, from sitting by the apartment pool with Margaret Fine-Manning.

And furthermore, David, who used to be so quiet and considerate, was turning mean. He asked Cheryl not to drive by so much, for instance, and he was sarcastic about her making slipcovers. "That's a perfect job for you," David said. "Just making pretty new covers to cover up old rotten furniture. Just covering it all up, that's all. Avoiding the issue."

Cheryl had stared at him—this conversation took place in broad daylight in the parking lot of the Swiss Chalet Apartments, in early June. "You must be thinking about upholstery," Cheryl had said. "I don't do that."

"Now listen to me," said Marie. "I'm trying to tell you something." She stood up and got more gin. "It's so satisfying to have a relationship with all the cards out on the table. *You don't have to be in love*, Cheryl, is what I'm trying to tell you. It's much better to have a relationship based on give-and-take, on honesty. No big promises, no big regrets. Pay as you go, cash 'n' carry, as Lenny says."

"I think that's awful," Cheryl said.

"Just *think* about it," insisted Marie. "His needs are met, your needs are met. A mature, *adult* relationship. You've got to shed this high school attitude and get out in the real world, Cheryl."

Cheryl sighed, stirring her drink with her fingers. She smiled to herself in the dark.

Because, speaking of high school, there was something that even Marie didn't know. Cheryl's mind went back to three days earlier at the hardware store, where she had gone to buy a new stakeout chain for Bob, he'd torn the old one up completely, you couldn't even imagine how.

Anyway, Cheryl had stepped up to the counter with Mary Duke in tow, and who should just happen to be there but Jerry Jarvis, the owner. Jerry Jarvis owned four stores now, he traveled from place to place. You rarely ever ran into him in town anymore.

"Hel-lo there!" Jerry had said. He ran his eyes over Cheryl and then slowly back over her again. Cheryl was feeling spacy and insubstantial—she wore shorts, that day.

"You're looking wonderful as always," Jerry Jarvis said. He probably hadn't realized how fat she'd been. Cheryl hadn't realized this either. "So how are things going?" he asked.

"Just fine," Cheryl said.

"Daddy left us and went to live in the Swiss Chalets," said Mary Duke.

Later, Cheryl could not figure out what had possessed the child. Normally Mary Duke was *too* quiet, and held too tight to your hand.

"I'm sorry to hear that," said Jerry Jarvis. But it was plain as day from the way his eyes lit up that he wasn't sorry at all. He'd always loved her—so he was glad! In fact, that very night he had called on the phone and asked Cheryl if she'd meet him at the bar at the Ramada Inn on Wednesday for a cocktail, he'd like to help her out in any way he could.

"Thanks but no thanks," Cheryl said then. "You're *married*."

While this was of course *true*, Jerry Jarvis admitted,

there were a lot of factors involved. He'd like to talk to her sometime, he'd like to explain these factors, that was all, he'd always thought so highly of Cheryl's opinion. Finally Cheryl had agreed to meet him at the Deli Box for lunch, sometime when she felt up to it. The Deli Box was right in the middle of town, it proved his good intentions, Cheryl guessed. She couldn't decide if she'd go or not.

Meanwhile a big truck had arrived the next day, from Jarvis Hardware and Building Supply, bringing a four-by-four wood frame and a load of sand to go in it. "For Mary Duke," he had written on his business card. "See you soon? Your Friend, Jerry Jarvis," as if she didn't know his last name! Cheryl had told the men to unload it in the corner of the backyard, where it sat right now, in fact, looming up whitely at them from the darkness beyond Bob on his stakeout chain.

"You need to meet some men," Marie was saying. "You ought to sign up for a course."

"Listen—" Cheryl said suddenly. "Listen here—" and she started at the beginning and told Marie all about Jerry Jarvis and the Deli Box and his sending the sand. "Isn't that *something*?" she asked at the end.

"Why, no," Marie said. "I think it's romantic."

"But he's *married*," Cheryl said.

"So what?" asked Marie. "He might be on the verge of a divorce, you never know. We call those 'men in transition' in my group," she said. "Anyway, you don't have to be in love with him. You can't marry anybody anyway, you haven't even got a divorce. Plus you've got all these children. It sounds to me like he's a real safe bet for you right now. I think you ought to go out with him."

"What?" Cheryl couldn't believe it.

"You know that old song?" said Marie.

"What old song?"

"Oh, you know the one I mean. It goes something about if you can't have the one you love, then love the one you're with."

"I think that's awful," said Cheryl. But she sat out in the lawn chair for a while longer, thinking about it and missing David, after Marie left in her Buick, bound for romance. Lenny was coming by later for a nightcap, so she said. Cheryl wondered what David was doing right now.

And then, in that way he had of anticipating you, of knowing just how you felt, Bob started to howl, low at first like a howl in her own head, and then louder until she took him off the chain and put him in the TV room.

This made Netta furious. "I work all day and what thanks do I get?" Netta said. "I can't even watch my program." Netta's program was *Dynasty*, which was on now. Netta had gotten bitchier and bitchier since she had started working for Lisa, who was real hard to work for. Cheryl sighed. She knew her mother was difficult too. Lisa said Netta insisted on sweeping up hair all the time instead of waiting until the girls were through for the day. It made both the girls and the customers nervous. But Netta said she couldn't stand to see that hair just laying all over the floor, she had to get it up. Then Lisa would yell at her, and then Netta would cry. It was really bad for business, Lisa had told Marie, to have your own mother in your shop crying and sweeping up hair. Now Netta was crying again. "Don't bring that dog in here," Netta begged. "Just let me watch my program in peace."

"I can't leave him out on the chain anymore, Mama," Cheryl said. "You can hear how he's started that howling. I guess I'll have to go ahead and hire Billy Majors to build him a pen."

Bob hung his head and scuttled sideways toward the sofa, panting.

"Well," Netta said. "Just do what you want to, then, you always do anyway, both you and your sister, Lisa."

"Mama," Cheryl said. It wasn't fair. They were driving her crazy. All of them: her mother and Lisa and Bob and the kids too, oh *especially* the kids, summer was awful with them out of school. Except for Louis, who had flunked ninth-grade math and Spanish—he'd almost flunked everything—and now had to take summer school. Meanwhile David just sat by the pool at the Swiss Chalet Apartments getting browner and younger-looking, with Margaret Fine-Manning. Cheryl didn't see how Margaret could get any sun at all on her legs, she had so much hair on them. It wasn't fair. Joan Collins got out of a car on TV,

Bob thumped his tail on the floor. "Good night, Mother," Cheryl said.

J uly was a busy month with a lot of things happening. The first one was that Louis passed math but flunked Spanish, and had to take it again in the second semester of summer school. The second thing was that Mr. and Mrs. Wright across the street, who had always acted so nice, showed their true colors at last. They started calling up on the telephone every time Bob howled and then they started calling the police. They swore out a warrant calling Bob a pernicious nuisance, which wasn't true at all, and enjoined him from howling. But Bob refused to be enjoined. If he stayed inside too long, he messed on the floor, but if he stayed outside on the chain too long, he howled. Cheryl was at her wits' end. So she called Billy Majors and asked him to build her a dog pen, and Billy Majors said okay, but she'd have to go to Jarvis Supply and sign for the materials.

As soon as Cheryl walked in the door she saw him, Jerry Jarvis, behind a big computer. He stood up right away and stared at Cheryl, hard, across the store. Their eyes locked. Then he came hurrying over and asked her what he could do for her today. Somehow what he said sounded dirty, and Cheryl blushed. "Oh, I didn't mean anything like *that*, honest, swear to God," Jerry said. Jerry had thinning red hair and beautiful big brown eyes.

Cheryl believed him. She believed that the reason he was still so crazy about her was that in all their years of dating they'd never actually done it. Cheryl had been so religious in high school, plus they all wore panty girdles in those days.

Now, Jerry was trying hard to make conversation. He asked her about playing tennis and Cheryl told him that no, she did not play tennis, and she needed to sign a note for whatever Billy Majors might require to build a pen for Bob.

"Billy Majors?" Jerry Jarvis acted amazed. He said he'd come over and build the pen himself, how about that?

Cheryl looked at his seersucker suit, his nice white shirt, his bright red tie. "No, Jerry, I don't think so," was all she said.

But later that same week, when the stuff from Jarvis Supply arrived, there was a new ornamental gate with wrought-iron flowers on it, and his business card saying "Pastrami on rye? Chicken on white? Your Friend, Jerry Jarvis."

Then Billy Majors, a high school dropout about Cheryl's age, came by and started Bob's pen. Luckily this kept Mary Duke and Bob both happy, someone in the backyard to talk to them. Cheryl was having trouble getting Angela to stay at home and babysit with Mary Duke—Angela kept hanging out at the mall where her boyfriend worked. Sandy was at day camp at the Y, thank God, but Louis was flunking Spanish in summer school.

Finally Cheryl, who didn't know any Spanish at all, went to see Louis's teacher in late July, to ask him if there was any way she could help Louis, anything they could do at home to improve his grade. His teacher turned out to be a short, stocky man with big liquid eyes and so much hair on his body that it curled out over his shirt collar. His name was Amerigo Ramirez, which sounded just like a country. Cheryl met him in his office at five P.M. on July 21, before a whirring fan. For a while they talked about Louis and Louis's attitude, which was a problem, Cheryl had to admit. Cheryl felt so hot she felt like she was bursting through her clothes. The fan went on and on. Mr. Ramirez gave her a list of verbs for Louis to learn. He gave her a record for Louis to listen to. Cheryl was hot, hot. It was hard to pay attention at all in this heat, surprising that the school had no air-conditioning. "Are there any problems at home?" asked Mr. Ramirez. Cheryl started crying. "Mrs. Stone, you are very attractive woman in my view," said Mr. Ramirez. His eyes were large and moist, he took off his shirt, Cheryl had never seen so much hair. Mr. Ramirez locked the door and redirected the fan to blow toward the green chenille-covered cot in his office. Cheryl went to bed with him there, that afternoon, while the football team drilled out on the field in the terrible heat. Cheryl could hear them grunting—"Ooh! Oof! Aah!"—like figures in a cartoon. She could hear the coach shout numbers at them through the hot, still air.

The following day, Mr. Ramirez sent her some roses

from Jo's Florist, but she wouldn't go out to dinner with him. She didn't think she'd see him again, because, as she told Marie, she just hadn't felt a thing. Nothing. Zero. Nothing like it had always been with David, from the word go.

David meanwhile had bought a Nissan station wagon and announced to them all that he and Margaret Fine-Manning were going to Maine, for their vacation. He gave Cheryl his itinerary, typed out. Bed-and-breakfasts, country inns.

"La-di-da," Netta said. "I'd sue his pants off if I was you."

But Cheryl and the kids went with Netta to the beach for a week, which is what they had always done every summer that Cheryl could remember, renting the very same house at Wrightsville Beach that they had rented for so many years. Before Cheryl's father died, before the children were born, before David left.

This year, the people who owned the house had installed a new outside shower and bought new redwood furniture for the porch. And even though the boys had a great time and Angela fell in love with a freshman from UNC, even though Purcell joined them for four days, the house seemed twice as large as it used to, way too big. The seashell wind chimes sounded so sad that Cheryl took them down. Netta ate shrimp every night. When Purcell was there, he caught crabs every day by dangling chicken necks on string from the end of the pier. While Louis and Sandy played endlessly in the endless surf, Cheryl lay on the beach and wept with her face hidden under a *People* magazine.

But she tanned easily, and the weather was perfect, and she looked terrific in her new bathing suit, cut up high on the sides of her legs. She'd lost seventeen pounds. Netta had started to say something about the bathing suit, but didn't. You could tell. Netta was being nice to Cheryl now since she wasn't speaking to Lisa, who had fired her from La Coiffure. Lisa said that Netta's crying and sweeping was ruining her business, her mother just had to go. Then when Netta had refused to quit, Lisa fired her. So Lisa and Netta were mad, and Lisa didn't come to the beach with them this year, but Marie did. Marie came down for a weekend while Lenny went to National Guard camp.

Marie said that everybody back home was talking about Netta and Lisa's big fight, some of them holding that Lisa had been wrong to fire her mother, and others that Lisa had been wronged by a mother who wouldn't act right. Everybody in town had an opinion. Cheryl and Marie rubbed coconut suntan lotion on their legs and talked about it. Cheryl couldn't decide what she thought. It seemed to her that Lisa had a point, but Netta had a point too. People must have stopped talking about her own separation by now, her separation must be old hat. This gave Cheryl a pang. She missed David. She did not miss Lisa, or Bob. With Bob in the kennel, Cheryl was getting a lot of rest.

Then Marie said that Angela had asked her to get her some birth control pills and she had said she'd do it, but she just thought Cheryl ought to know. So Cheryl had *that* to think about too. She and Marie lay back on the sand, smelling like big sweet tropical drinks.

Netta came out of the house then, wearing a flowered robe and a big-brimmed hat, smoking a cigarette, picking her way toward them through the sand. It took her a while to get there. For the first time it struck Cheryl how old her mother looked, and how crazy. Netta was starting to look like Mamaw, who had been dead for years and years. Netta said she was going to take Mary Duke over to the water slide, which she had been doing every day. For some reason Mary Duke had decided on this trip that she didn't like the ocean, and she wouldn't go near it with a ten-foot pole. So Mary Duke was staying mostly in the house watching TV and driving everybody crazy.

"I don't see how she can be afraid of the ocean and not afraid of the water slide," Marie said.

"She thinks there's things in the ocean," Cheryl said. "You know—*Jaws*."

Netta leaned across Cheryl and tapped Marie on the knee. "Did you hear how my own daughter Lisa did me?" she asked, and Marie said yes, she had heard it all right.

Then Netta grabbed Cheryl's knee so hard Cheryl sat up. Netta's face beneath the huge hat brim was pale and trembly. "You wouldn't do that, would you, honey?" she asked.

"Do what, Mama?" Cheryl said.

"Get rid of me like that, you know, for no reason."

"No," Cheryl said. "Of course not." It was true.

"Grammy, Grammy," Mary Duke called from the house. Netta straightened up and started across the sand.

"My whole body feels different since I've been having this relationship with Lenny," Marie began. "It's hard to explain."

Cheryl lay flat on her back in the warm sand, smelling sweet and staring straight up at the hot white sun.

*G*reat tan," Jerry Jarvis said. The way he said it sounded suggestive, but then when she thought about it later, Cheryl was not so sure. Maybe he didn't mean to sound that way, maybe he was just being nice after all. Certainly it was nice of him to stop by like this after work to check out the dog pen and see how things were going. Not so well, was the truth, which she didn't say. Bob had grown bigger and stronger at the kennel while they were away, and now he kept digging out of his pen despite the pretty ornamental gate that Jerry had sent over, despite the rocks and boards and things that Cheryl and the kids kept piling around the bottom of the fence to keep him in. The week before, Cheryl had bought a whole truckload of cinder blocks, and every time he got out, she'd put a cinder block where he did it, or a big rock she lugged up from the creek. It went on and on. Last Thursday when Bob got out, he went two streets over and stole a three-by-five Oriental rug from the Lucases, who had just moved down here from Fairfax, Virginia. Another time he knocked over Mr. Ellman's brother, who had a pacemaker.

Now Bob bounded against the fence, in high spirits. Cheryl sighed. She knew he could get out anytime he wanted to, until she got something along every inch of that pen. Every inch. Bob was such a hassle, but Cheryl couldn't bring herself to consider getting rid of him, she couldn't have told you why. And now Margaret Fine-Manning had moved in with David and they jogged together every morning. They ran from the Swiss Chalets all the way to Burger King, along the highway. Cheryl, driving to work, saw them every day. Margaret wore ankle weights.

"Cheryl?" Jerry Jarvis was saying. "Listen to me."

Cheryl looked at him. His hair was red, his face was flushed, and his eyes were as blue as the sky. He was a big, impressive man. "I can have a boy over here tomorrow to run you a little old electric wire right around the bottom of this fence and then you won't have no more trouble. It won't hurt him a bit. Just a little jolt is all, he won't hardly feel it, but I guarantee you he'll stay in this pen."

"Well, thanks, Jerry," Cheryl said, "but I think that's awful. Shocking him."

"Wouldn't hurt him a bit, now," Jerry said. He grinned at her. He had big, white, even teeth, and Cheryl found herself grinning back.

"No," she said. "I know you think it's stupid, but I won't do that. I'll just keep on doing what I'm doing. We'll just put more stuff around until he can't get out, that's all. Sandy would have a fit if Bob got electric shock."

"It's not *electric shock*, Cheryl." Jerry was laughing. "It's really nothing, just a little whammy, that's it."

"No," Cheryl said.

She stood by the fancy gate as Jerry Jarvis walked over to his hardware truck. Sometimes he drove the truck, and sometimes he drove his BMW. It was September now, almost time for school to start. The leaves on the hickory tree looked papery against the sky, yellowing. Cheryl felt cold suddenly, although it wasn't cold. She couldn't think why she was being so silly about this pen.

Jerry Jarvis reached his truck and opened the door and then suddenly slammed it. He turned and walked back to her, fast. He grabbed her and pulled her to him and crushed her up against his yellow shirt. "Cheryl, Cheryl," he said. "I've got to have you, it's only a matter of time."

"Let go of me this minute, Jerry Jarvis," Cheryl said.

"You're driving me crazy," said Jerry Jarvis.

Then he kissed Cheryl slow and hard, a kiss that left

her breathless, leaning against Bob's pen. Jerry rubbed her cheek and smiled into her eyes, it was clear he didn't even care who might be looking. "You know where to call me if you want me," he said.

Then Jerry Jarvis sent her twelve free cinder blocks, but he didn't come back again. School started. Cheryl was swamped with orders for slipcovers—fall was very big in the slipcover business. Angela cut off all her hair except for one long piece down the back, which she dyed pink. Lisa almost died when she saw how Angela looked. But Angela liked it. Cheryl didn't know what to think about Angela's hair—at least Angela's old boyfriend, Scott Eubanks, had gotten busted for marijuana over the summer and had been sent to live with his father in Georgia, so that was something. Cheryl guessed she could stand Angela's hair. And Louis had started off better in school this year. He liked English. Of course he had passed Spanish, after all. Sandy too was doing better—he'd stopped coughing, for one thing, and his Cub Scout troop had a new leader who was young and energetic. Sandy had earned merit badges in knot tying, carpentry, and letter writing. For his letter-writing badge, Sandy had to write a hundred letters. He had a Cub Scout pen pal in England who wrote to him on thin crinkly blue see-through paper. Sandy had also written several letters to his father, which just killed Cheryl. She couldn't imagine what in the world he said.

Also, Sandy had a new friend named Olan Barker who had moved in with his family up the street. So Sandy was doing better, all in all, and his interest in Bob had waned. Oh, Sandy still patted him, and fed him sometimes, but he never took Bob walking—and in all fairness to Sandy, he almost *couldn't*. For Bob had grown and grown. Sandy couldn't control him. Bob had become Cheryl's dog, finally, totally, after all. And sometimes he still got out of his pen: He'd move a cinder block, tunnel out, and run wild until somebody called the police, who came and got him and put him in the pound.

This happened in late September. When Cheryl went down to the police station to get him, the officer in charge was very friendly. At first he said there'd be a forty-two-dollar fine and then when Cheryl looked stunned to hear that—it was the end of the month, she wouldn't get paid till the first, and David had paid only half his child support for reasons he hadn't explained—when she looked so depressed, the officer in charge said, well, nobody was there but them, and why didn't he just tear up the ticket like this?—he tore it up before her eyes and dropped it in the basket by his desk—and he'd issue Bob a warning instead. He filled out the warning on a green card and handed it to her.

This officer was young, blond, and plump, with a big wide smile. He said that actually he didn't give a damn, that he didn't think the police ought to have to deal with dogs anyway, that every other town he'd ever heard of had a dogcatcher. He said this was a one-horse town in his opinion, with no nightlife. He said he was from Gainesville, Florida. He wore a badge that said "M. Herron," so Cheryl guessed this was his name. She looked around the police station, and he was right. Nobody else was there at all.

The police station used to be the agriculture extension office. She'd had 4-H in here. The gray painted concrete floor was exactly the same. Almost the only way you could tell it was a police station now was by the messiness of it—cigarette butts jabbed down in sand-filled containers, paper cups on the floor. The county extension agent, Louise Gore, would never have allowed this disorder. Cheryl remembered Miss Gore's tight yellow curls and how particular she was about buttonholes. It was right here, all those years ago, that Cheryl had started sewing. She'd made an apron, an overblouse, a Christmas-tree skirt with felt appliqués. Now wanted posters hung on the wall, full-face and profile: One man, bearded, looked like David. Or she thought he did.

Cheryl, daydreaming, was so confused that when M. Herron offered to pick up Bob at the dog pound and bring him home after he got off duty, she said yes. Later she realized she should have said no. But by then it was too late. And when M. Herron showed up just at dark in his police car, it was real exciting. Clearly, Bob was glad to be home. He barked and lunged at them all and rolled on the grass.

It took Cheryl, M. Herron, and Louis all working together to catch him and put him back on the stakeout chain, where he'd have to stay until Cheryl could get his pen fixed.

Then M. Herron let Mary Duke and Sandy get in the police car and showed them how everything worked. They even got to talk to headquarters on the radio, and M. Herron drove them around the block with the blue light flashing. He told Netta he loved children. When he finally left, Angela said he was cute. "Ha!" Netta said.

M. Herron came back on Tuesday, Cheryl's morning off, to give them some free burglar-prevention advice which he said they needed. By coincidence, Netta was not at home, having gone to the outlet mall. M. Herron was not wearing his uniform. He walked through every inch of their house checking doors and windows and then advised Cheryl to go right out and buy deadbolt locks. "You can't be too careful," he said.

Cheryl went to bed with him in her own bed, and after it was over, she got up and went in the bathroom and took a shower and then came back and saw M. Herron still there in her bed, against the yellow sheets. She thought he'd be dressed, but he wasn't. All he wore was a gold neck-chain. He held out his arms to Cheryl and said he wanted to give her a big kiss. Then he said he hated to brag, but he was a pretty good cook, and wouldn't she like to come over for dinner on Saturday? He said he lived at the Swiss Chalets. "Well, thanks," Cheryl said without batting an eye—she was proud of herself, later on—"but actually I have a long-term relationship with a dentist in Raleigh and I can't do this anymore. I guess you just swept me right off my feet," she said.

By late October, Lisa and Netta were reconciled. Purcell, who had a lot of influence in community affairs, had helped Netta get a job at the new Council on Aging, which had just opened its office downtown in the courthouse. This job suited Netta to a tee. It was as good as the liquor store had been for seeing people, but nothing about it made her nervous, the way watching the hair pile up around the chairs and not sweeping it up did. Netta had a list of practical nurses, maids, and companions for the elderly, and she matched them up with names of older people who needed help. Also, she organized craft classes, gourmet cooking classes, genealogy classes, etc. Netta loved her job. She said it made her feel young again.

David told the kids that Margaret was pregnant and that he and Margaret were "delighted" by this news. But they did not plan to marry, he said. He said marriage was an outmoded concept in his and Margaret's opinion.

"I bet she doesn't *want* to marry him," Marie said. "She just wants to have a baby with a smart father. A lot of women get like that, they hear the biological clock just ticking away."

Cheryl was astonished. This idea—that Margaret might not want to marry David—had not occurred to her. She thought that David didn't want to marry Margaret, or he would. Or he would do it when the divorce became final, next spring.

"You better watch out now, honey," Purcell said. "He's liable to come traipsing back here with his tail between his legs, any day now. You'd better get yourself a game plan," Purcell said.

But Cheryl didn't have one.

All she did was go to work, and come home again, glad to have a permanent job now since Johnnie Sue had had her baby and it was colicky so she had decided not to return to Fabric World after all. Cheryl made $160 a week, plus whatever extra she got for slipcovers, which would be un-limited if she had the time and the energy. She had more orders than she could ever fill; it looked like the sky was the limit in the slipcover business. Lisa had suggested that Cheryl ought to hire some other women to sew them, say three or four women, and then Cheryl could just take the measurements and order the cloth and pay the women by the hour and make a big profit. "You can start your own business," Lisa said. "You can quit working at Fabric World and make a mint." This was a great idea and Cheryl knew it. But for some reason she was dragging her feet, losing orders. Maybe she didn't want to have her own business. Maybe she didn't want to be like Lisa. Maybe . . . oh, who knows?

Anyway, Cheryl had her hands full, what with the chil-dren, and Netta, and the slipcovers she'd promised, and Bob. She was stitching a mauve sofa cover for Mr. and Mrs.

Holden Bench one Saturday night in early November, just after Halloween, when Bob got out again. She couldn't believe it. But she should have known. First, he'd howled and howled, and then he had fallen suddenly, mysteriously silent, and now here he was barking, and jumping against the front door. Cheryl stopped stitching and turned off the light on her machine. She stood up. "Louis, Sandy—" she yelled, and then stopped. Her voice echoed through the empty rooms of this house that she had lived in all her life. Too late she remembered that she was here by herself tonight. Everybody was gone—everybody in the whole world, it suddenly seemed. Angela was off on a date, Netta was out playing rook with the New Generation card group, Sandy had gone on a Cub Scout camping trip, Louis was at the movies seeing *Rambo* for the fourth time, and Mary Duke was spending the night with her friend Catherine. Cheryl was home alone. She remembered M. Herron and what he had said about nightlife, and burglars.

Cheryl opened the kitchen door and Bob bounded in, wagging his tail so hard that it crashed him into the refrigerator, then into the kitchen table, where her sewing machine was set up. "Now you just come right along here," she said firmly, grasping his collar, dragging him through the kitchen away from the mauve sailcloth all over the kitchen floor, toward the TV room. Bob reared back on his haunches and allowed himself to be scooted along. Cheryl gritted her teeth, dragging Bob. She would fix that pen right now, right this minute, by herself. And he'd stay in it. She shut Bob in the TV room and turned on *The Love Boat* to keep him quiet.

Cheryl put on a dark flannel shirt and a woolen cap. She felt like a burglar herself. She took off her loafers and put on some of Angela's boots. She got the flashlight out of the laundry room and went out the back door. Lord, it was cold! A chilly, gusty wind came whipping along, kicking up all the leaves. You could smell wood smoke in the air, and something else. Cheryl couldn't quite place what it was. Something cold, something sharp, it reminded her of winter. Winter was on the way. The almost-bare limbs of the hickory tree showed black against the full yellow moon and then disappeared when the moon popped in and out of the puffy dark clouds that ran across it. Cheryl's own backyard seemed unfamiliar, a scary but enchanted place—full of moving light and darkness, wind—and she remembered M. Herron saying a lady can't be too careful. But that was ridiculous. She could do it. Of course if she had let Jerry Jarvis send a man over here, this pen would have been foolproof months ago. But Cheryl could do it herself, and she would.

With the flashlight, she walked the fence until she found the spot where Bob had tunneled under. Then she walked back to the garage and got the last cinder block and carried it balanced against her stomach and placed it carefully in the hole. There now. And that ought to do it too, she thought, flashing the light around the bottom of the fence. There, now.

Cheryl went into the house and got Bob and dragged him across the kitchen and pulled him across the yard to his pen and pushed him inside, latching the ornamental gate securely. She felt flushed, and strong, and ready for anything, the cold night air so pleasant on her cheeks that she couldn't bear the idea of going back in and working on the Benches' slipcover. Instead, Cheryl went to the kitchen and got three California Coolers out of the refrigerator and opened one of them and turned off the kitchen light and went back out and sat down in a lawn chair.

The wind and the shadows moved all around her, she felt like she glowed in the dark. The dry leaves rustled at her feet, red and brown and gold, but she couldn't see their colors, only feel them in the dark. It was true she was artistic, she did have a sense of color, maybe she'd open up a business after all. Bob barked, then rattled the leaves, then made a snuffling, scuffling noise. Cheryl opened another California Cooler, she knew he was digging out. It's only a matter of time, she thought, he's digging out. She imagined David and Margaret Fine-Manning entertaining M. Herron right now at a gourmet dinner in their apartment at the Swiss Chalets, she saw the candlelight gleaming in David's eyes, and the gleam of M. Herron's gold neck-chain. The moon went in and out, in and out of the tumbling clouds. Cheryl imagined Jerry Jarvis unhappily at home with his fat wife, Darlene. She imagined Marie and Lenny embracing in a motel in Gatlinburg, Tennessee, where they went this weekend to look at the leaves. Cheryl leaned back in her chair and opened the third California Cooler and laughed out loud finally as Bob scraped out and shook himself off and lurched over to stand for a minute there by her chair before he took off running free across the darkened yards, beneath the yellow moon.

Mom

Right before the police came looking for Buddy the first time, Gloria knew something was up. Or she sort of knew it, or she didn't know she knew it, or something. Today she feels that way again. Ms. Ferebee-Bunch says Gloria was in denial then. Maybe so. Or maybe she's just psychic. But Ms. Ferebee-Bunch says it is a family illness, and Gloria is sick too. Gloria doesn't buy this for one minute! There's nothing wrong with *her.* Buddy started running with the wrong crowd, that's all. But what can you expect? It's a jungle out there. Gloria moves over to the window and looks out at the Nu-Tread Tire Co. which is just letting out, it's six o'clock. Dinnertime. This whole neighborhood is going down. Trash on the streets, abandoned houses, you name it. It didn't used to be this way. Gloria remembers when Buddy was real little and she'd take him to the park for the whole day, and nobody ever bothered them at all. The park was full of kids and old people then. She remembers how Buddy used to organize the other kids into teams for his own complicated games, games he made up. He was a natural leader, his teachers always said so. Gloria stares out the window. She clutches her pocketbook, nice white patent leather. She's got to go to the Safeway. On the other hand she feels so funny, like something's up, like something's going to happen. She's always been real tuned in to things, she really could've been a psychic if she'd had the training. Then she wouldn't have to work so damn hard. She could just hang out a sign and let people come to *her*, like Ms. Ferebee-Bunch. Gloria fiddles with her pocketbook, looking out the window.

And then, sure enough, the phone rings.

"Mrs. Anderson?" The man has no accent, like a newsman on TV.

"Yes?" Gloria says. One of the guys leaving Nu-Tread waves at her, and Gloria waves back.

"Mrs. Anderson, this is Leonard Sauls," he says. "I'm afraid I have some bad news for you."

Gloria sits down on the couch. She *knew* it!

"Your son Buddy left the group this morning during an outing," the man continues. "We took them out to the park. They were going to learn something about rock climbing, before the trip we wrote to you about. Anyway, on the hike back to the van, Buddy just vanished."

"What do you mean, 'vanished'?"

"Disappeared into the trees. It was the damnedest thing. He was just gone."

"Did he say anything?" Gloria manages to ask. "To any of the other kids, I mean."

"If he did, they're not talking. We have notified the police, of course. They'll be checking the bus stations and the highway between here and Raleigh. If you hear from him, call the police immediately. If you get him, call us. And in the meantime, we'll let *you* know, the minute we hear anything." For the first time, his voice softens a little.

Gloria says good-bye. Thanks. She had a feeling in her bones, as Mamaw would have said. Buddy's been saying all along that people are mean to him in the group home. He's had a tone in his voice. She'd better not go to the Safeway. She'd better sit right here by the phone awhile and see if Buddy calls her. Buddy's been saying the food at the group home is awful too. He never was a good eater, as a child. He just liked certain things, such as Hawaiian Punch and bacon. He's real sensitive too. Gloria's heart swells—she's close to tears. She gets a Dixie cup full of champagne, which she buys at the Safeway, which is one reason she was going over there. Gloria used to actually drink, back when her and Richard first split up and she'd just started dating again after being married ever since she was a teenager. But now she doesn't really drink anymore. All she ever has is a little Dixie cup of champagne, for nerves.

Gloria looks in the phone book. Then she writes the

police emergency number, 911, down on a recipe card. She lays down on the couch and puts the phone on her stomach, the recipe card under the phone, and the bottle of André beside her on the floor. When Buddy calls her, she's supposed to call the cops. They've gone over all that with her. But she might as well relax awhile now. Isn't this what the social worker said, that you need to work on yourself? You can't control other people, you have to let them go. Ms. Ferebee-Bunch said that too. You must let other people face the consequences of their actions. What a laugh, since most people get off scot-free. Look at Richard for instance. Ms. Ferebee-Bunch is a bitch. Also, she has not got any figure at all, she looks like an ironing board. Very carefully, Gloria refills the Dixie cup and lays back down to relax and think about things. But so much stuff has happened that now she can't remember exactly what happened when. It all runs together in her head.

Certain times do stick out in her memory, though, like those dolls at the fair that keep popping up and you're supposed to whack them back down with a sledgehammer. Buddy used to love that game. Gloria took him to the state fair every single year, she liked it as much as he did. One time they both got sick on the pirate ship after eating some kind of weird food cooked by people from a foreign land. The state fair is full of culture, you'd be surprised. Gloria can close her eyes right now and see herself and Buddy, running up the midway, holding hands so they won't get lost from each other. Buddy had real blond hair then. Now it's turned dark, though. The fair is expensive but Gloria made sure he got to go every year, the same way she made sure he got a Big Wheel when he was little, or a BMX bike, or whatever. Later, stone-washed jeans and Reeboks. Gloria didn't mind going without, to get him whatever he wanted. She really didn't. She was glad to do it, that's the way she is. She's always been too big-hearted for her own good, she'll tell you that herself.

But she kind of wishes these moments would quit popping up like they do. You have to live in the present tense, everybody knows that. Gloria looks at the phone and remembers answering it all those times in the past, and voices—often a deep man's voice, not a boy's—would say, "Is Buddy there?" or, "Can I speak to Buddy?" and if she said he wasn't home right then, the line went dead. Nobody ever left a message. And Gloria'd stand holding the phone, with her stomach feeling funny and her hand sweating on the receiver. Of course Buddy was always real popular. He had lots of friends. She couldn't expect to know them all. Lots of girlfriends too—boys will be boys, after all! You've got to give a boy some growing room.

And the fact is, Gloria works nights anyway—hostess at the Texas Grill, a fancier place than you'd think from the sound of it, Tex-Mex is big now, even in Raleigh—so she never knew if he kept his curfew or not. Another moment that keeps popping up, though, is the first time she went in Buddy's room and found him gone, and his bed not even slept in! He hadn't even bothered to pull the sheet down. Gloria always tried not to go in his room too much, or look around too much when she was in there. Before he quit school, though, she had to wake him up every morning or he'd never make it, and he'd talk so hateful then—yet he was just an angel as a child. "Angel child," Gloria used to call him.

Now Buddy's language is awful, he gets it from the culture, though. Just look at Madonna on TV! It's a wonder anybody ever grows up alive, in Gloria's opinion. Plus the divorce, of course. Lord knows, Gloria tried to make up for not having a daddy in place, so to speak, but it was hard. You can give till you're blue in the face, but there's nobody home to play catch with, that's a fact. Of course she *did* try real hard to work it out with her boyfriend John—now that would have been great because he was so manly and everything—but Gloria can still remember Buddy's little face with his bottom lip all stuck out whenever John would tell him to do something. John was just too bossy! John had a personality problem. He thought he could move in here and just *take over*, of course he was career Army so you can see why he felt that way. Now John owns two Mister Boston Pizzas, he could have given Buddy a good job too. Maybe Gloria could have been a hostess at Mister Boston. She can just see herself now, in a little red dress with an apron, and John in a red dinner jacket, and Buddy in a white shirt with a bow tie, waiting on tables at Mister Boston. Too bad it didn't work out!

Too bad his father moved all the way up to Asheville

too, you can't be any kind of a male model from a distance of four hours away. Anyway, Richard was just *too* strict, he had a poker up his ass, as Mamaw always said. Remember how mad he got when Mamaw wouldn't take care of herself anymore and Gloria had to move her in with them, that was in the duplex over in Bellaire Gardens when Gloria was pregnant, maybe it wasn't a great way to start a marriage but there was nobody else to take care of Mamaw so Gloria had to do it, didn't she? Somebody had to do it!

And Gloria's been taking care of people since she was born. Or she feels like it, anyway. Mamaw just couldn't get it together after Pop died, so Gloria had to do *everything* for herself and her little sister, Tonette. Now Tonette is an interior decorator in Atlanta, with an answer phone. A *designer*, she calls herself. She won't hardly speak to her sister, even though she wouldn't've had a thing if it wasn't for Gloria and how Gloria took such good care of her, all those years of their childhood. Why, Gloria spent her own money on Tonette's dancing lessons. What was it Ann Landers said? *If you act like a rug, somebody's going to walk on you.* This is the story of Gloria's life.

So Richard got mad about Mamaw living with them. But Richard is the kind of man that if it isn't one thing, it's another. For instance, he used to keep a little notebook in the car where he'd write down mileage and when he filled the car up and where, so he'd know how many miles to the gallon he was getting. Gloria couldn't ever see why he wanted to know this information—she couldn't see why it was important. Richard is an insurance executive, which figures. He used to love to plan for the future, he'd write down his plans in the order of their priority: 1, 2, 3, 4. In fact, Richard used to drive Gloria just crazy in general, but the funny thing is, she's missed him ever since they split up. In a kind of weird way, but still . . . she can't explain it. One time about five years ago, right after John left her and before Richard remarried, Gloria sort of mentioned this to Richard on the phone.

She will never forget what he said: "Gloria, life as we knew it is a thing of the past."

Richard actually said this! He used to call her his little sunshine. Now he lives in a white brick house overlooking a golf course with his new wife, Barbara (a bitch), and her two little boys, who wear white shorts and knit shirts and take tennis lessons all the time according to Buddy. For the past two years, Buddy has refused to see his father at all. So Richard is not any kind of a male model for him now. And still he has the nerve to say she's spoiled Buddy—*spoiled* him, when all Richard ever did was criticize her and then leave them both! It's just a damn good thing she was willing to take on all that responsibility, she ought to get some thanks for it too.

The only thing Richard does now is pay that child support for Buddy on the first of every month, and that will stop next year, when he turns eighteen. Richard won't pay a penny then, he's already said so. "If he can get himself straightened out and he wants to go to college," Richard said over the phone, "he can let me know. Tell him to call my secretary and make an appointment." He slammed down the phone. Gloria can't see how he can be so hard-hearted to his own flesh and blood. Since he moved up to Asheville, he acts more and more like a Yankee.

Another moment that keeps popping up in Gloria's mind took place just before the judge sent Buddy off to the group home. She woke Buddy up one Saturday morning and said, "Okay, surprise, we're going to drive down to Morehead City and eat some seafood at Captain Bill's, spend the night, have a good time on the beach." She was nervous about waking him up—she didn't want him to yell at her. But Buddy sat up and looked out at her calmly from under all his hair. He was getting so thin. "Mom, you've got to be kidding," he said.

"No, Woodrow, I'm not," Gloria said, using his real name for some reason, surprised to find herself so close to tears, and maybe Buddy picked up on this because he got right up without too much grumbling. They went in her old Dodge Dart, a car like a tank, but dependable, at least it had air-condition. Gloria threaded her way through south Raleigh and finally got on the Beltline, then onto 70. "Thank goodness, no more traffic!" she said brightly into the rearview mirror, but by then Buddy was sound asleep.

It was one in the afternoon. Gloria twisted around so she could see him better. Buddy looked a little bit like Jeff Bridges, Gloria can remember his father, Lloyd Bridges, in *Sea Hunt*! Or was that the name of it? It was all about underwater. Buddy slept with his mouth slightly open, his head turned to the side. Occasionally he made a funny little snuffly noise. When he was little, he used to have bad dreams, he'd toss and turn and cry out in his sleep, then sometimes he'd get up and run into Gloria's room and snuggle up in bed with her. Gloria always loved the way he smelled, like a puppy. She loved his little milk-breath.

As she drove down 70 toward the beach with Buddy sleeping in the back, all arms and legs and angles, Gloria was happier than she had been in months. For once she knew where he was! He was here, with her, just like he used to be, the two of them closed in against the world which flew past hot and wild, neon signs and barbecue joints, ninety degrees in the shade. She remembered earlier trips they'd made to the beach, ages before, riding with Richard when Buddy was little and Richard wouldn't stop for the bathroom, he made Buddy pee in a mason jar. Gloria drove sixty-five mph down Route 70 with Buddy sleeping so soundly that she found herself talking out loud to him, it didn't matter since he couldn't hear her anyway, he was asleep. She told him about those earlier trips with his daddy, and about funny things he used to say when he was little. She loved how his face looked in sleep, slack-jawed and wholly open, innocent and defenseless, young. He is still her little boy. He will always be her little boy, no matter how old he gets, no matter what he does. Gloria remembers the valentine that Buddy made for her in fifth grade, and the way he turned the money from his paper route over to her for groceries. She wouldn't take it, of course. She wanted him to spend it on himself. And now as Gloria thinks about that day of driving out Route 70 to the beach, it seems to stretch out, to last forever, Gloria and Buddy in the old Dodge Dart, with the windows up, the air-condition on. It didn't last forever, of course, and what happened at the beach is something she'd rather forget, frankly.

As she would rather forget the time she found that tool—what do you call it? The long thin kind you use to open your car door when you've locked your keys inside. But as Gloria told Ms. Ferebee-Bunch, she just didn't think anything about it at the time. She was much more surprised at finding Buddy home in the middle of the day with two older boys—in her own apartment, when she thought he was in school! And she was much more upset about these friends of Buddy's than about whatever they might have brought along with them. A Negro might have anything, it's no way to tell what one might bring into your home.

Gloria said all this to Ms. Ferebee-Bunch, who did not bat an eye. She just looked at Gloria, cold as ice. Maybe Ms. Ferebee-Bunch has some Negro blood herself, a little touch of it like Dinah Shore, because she is the one that recommended for Buddy to go to the group home.

It's dark now. The neon lights have come on in the Nu-Tread tire sign. The André's all gone. Gloria sits up and stares at the index card.

She needs to go on out to the Safeway before it closes, but she needs to be here to answer the phone. Also, she needs to cash a check, this is another problem. She can't think what to do. Plus that new man in the apartment upstairs has got the flu, so she was going to get him something good to eat when she went out, maybe a Sara Lee coffee cake. Everybody likes Sara Lee. Suddenly the phone shrills out. It sounds so loud in this silent apartment. It startles Gloria so much that she knocks the receiver off the couch, trying to answer it.

"Hello?" she says. "Hello?" But all she hears is breathing, then a click on the end of the line. The receiver buzzes in her hand. Wrong number. Carefully she replaces it and settles back on the couch. It'll ring again in a minute. It'll be Buddy. He'll need some food, he'll want some money. And now, all of a sudden, Gloria knows what she'll say. Ms. Ferebee-Bunch can go to hell. *Sure, honey,* she'll say. *Yes. Come on home.* Gloria remembers the time when Buddy was a Wise Man in the kindergarten play. She dressed him up in a blue plaid robe, but the kindergarten teacher made him wear a plain navy robe, somebody else's, instead. They didn't have plaid in Jesus' time, the teacher said. It's going to ring any minute now. It'll be Buddy. He's a good boy. He will go to college, he will be a big shot, he will take such good care of his mother. The phone on Gloria's stomach rises and falls with her breath.

Life on the Moon

For Susan Raines

This story starts at the National Air and Space Museum in our nation's capital, with me and Lucie taking the Beginner Space Quiz and Richie and Tommy (her little boy) running wild all over the place while Darnell held on tight to my hand. I guess I ought to say something about the Air and Space Museum, I don't know if you've been there or not. It is a huge beautiful building all glass and concrete, with real planes hanging from its high ceiling and rockets and things all over the place. Then you can go in any of the exhibits and learn about something in particular—hot-air balloons, World War I, you name it. Wilbur and Orville Wright's plane, the first one, hangs right up at the front where you go in, and it is so tiny you can't imagine how it ever got off of the ground. It's the littlest thing in the whole museum. But anyway this museum is like the biggest room you ever saw, full of color and noise and flight. It made Richie and Tommy crazy like they wanted to fly themselves, they wouldn't stay with us or watch any of those programs all the way through. "Let them go," Lucie said, which I did because there wasn't anything else to do, no point to try to keep them if they wouldn't stay.

Now this museum had another effect on Darnell, more like it had on me. It made her hunch her shoulders and press real hard against my side. And me? It made me want to shrink too, pull in my feet and arms for fear they would touch something foreign and cold and made of some material you never would find on this earth, something slimy you didn't know what it was. At the same time it made my head sort of float up off of my body—the way I get in malls ever since Lonnie left me—like I was talking and hearing myself talk at the same time, or walking and watching myself walk, or taking the Space Quiz with Lucie and watching myself do it while I did.

First thing we did was press the button that said MIN-IMUM DIFFICULTY.

The square green letters came out on the screen like on a computer.

WHAT PLANET, they read, MOST CLOSELY RESEMBLES THE EARTH?

"Venus," Lucie said right away.

CORRECT, the machine spelled out. NUMBER TWO. WHAT PLANET IS FARTHEST FROM THE SUN?

"Mama, I have to go to the bathroom." Darnell pulled at my hand.

"Mercury," I said, but we missed whether that was right or not because Richie and Tommy came up right then with their faces looking like Christmas, to tell us that the Lunar Module was at the other end of the building, the real thing, they said, and we had to come right away.

"I have to go to the bathroom," Darnell said again, but Richie punched her.

"Listen," he said. "The astronauts peed in their suits."

"You quit that," I told Richie from my mouth which floated away up high in my face above us all. I could look down and see us and see all the tourists from foreign lands.

WHAT PLANET IS CHARACTERIZED BY RINGS? the machine spelled out, and Richie and Tommy together hollered out, "Saturn!"

Darnell was crying.

"Come on, then," Lucie said.

She moved off easily through the saris, the backpacks and blue jeans and car coats, looking like a foreigner herself with her jeans and those running shoes. I think you should dress for a trip myself, but I have to say that by then my feet were hurting from my heels.

After the bathroom, where we had to stand in line with French people and I had to put toilet paper all around the seat for Darnell, you can't be too careful, we finally made it to the other end of the museum, where Lucie stood reading the sign by the Lunar Module and Richie and Tommy jumped all around.

Lucie turned her face to me then, that same dark quick fairy-tale face she had as a little child, and took my hand.

"Oh, June," she said. "Oh, June, don't you remember? Oh, June, aren't you glad you came?"

Well, I was. I still am. But it was a bigger trip than you can imagine by a long shot.

When Lonnie left me, all I did for two weeks was throw up and cry. Oh, I was plenty mad too. Everything that happened made me sick or mad or sometimes all of it, like when I went down to the mall to get some panty hose at Belk's and when they were out of my size I had to get a paper bag from the salesgirl and breathe in it right there in the middle of the hosiery department to keep from passing out. Then I went into the ladies' and threw up. Another time I was walking through the Montgomery Ward TV section, about two hundred of those TVs were on and there was a bowl game with Bear Bryant in full color on every one, wearing his hat. Lonnie loved TV football, he loved the Bear. I used to get mad at him for watching and try to make him look at educational things on Channel 6. I wanted to expand his horizons, as Lucie said when she ran off with the disc jockey. But Lord, it made me cry, I had to tear out of Montgomery Ward and over to The Green Thumb and hide behind the ferns to collect myself. I lost eleven pounds the first two weeks.

Meanwhile Richie and Darnell were shooting down spaceships on the Atari that Lonnie had given them for Christmas, shooting down ship after ship. Lonnie just spoiled them to death, he always did, gave them everything they wanted and then some. They did that for one week solid, while they were out of school for Christmas; then they started skating their new skateboards straight through the family room, where Lonnie had taken the rug and the E-Z Boy recliner, and I never said one word. This was not like me, you can be sure. It's not the way I am about a house.

Lonnie took the rug and the E-Z Boy and his clothes and six pieces of Tupperware, that's all, and moved in with a nurse from the hospital, Sharon Ledbetter, into her one-bedroom apartment at Colony Courts. He met her at the hospital, I found out later, last year when Richie had his tonsils out. So I guess it had gone on since then, and I never knew a thing.

Sharon Ledbetter is twenty-three years old. *It is trite*, I thought of saying, but Lonnie would not have even known what that meant, so why bother? *Why bother?* I asked myself. You can subscribe to the *National Geographic* for ten years straight, but there are some people who won't do a thing except look at the naked pictures.

Richie and Darnell went over to visit the apartment at Colony Courts and came back saying that Sharon Ledbetter had a cat named Ms. Pacman and a whole lot of terrific rock albums which she was going to tape for them. They had a real good time. Now right after this was when my first cousin Lucie called from Alexandria where she lives and said why didn't I and the children come up to Washington and sightsee, it would be good for all of us to get away. She knew what a hard time I was having, Lucie said.

"Thanks but no thanks," I told her. "I'm too busy trying to put my life in order again," I said, and Lucie said she knew I was good at *that*, she wished me the best, but I ought to remember that sometimes it just isn't possible to do it right away. At this point I started to cry. I have never approved of Lucie and the way she left her own little boy down here with her mama to raise, in fact for years Lucie has made me real nervous.

"Come on, Mama, let's go to Washington," Richie said. Richie is always right there at your elbow when you think he's not, he never misses a trick. He's a redhead like his daddy, into something every minute of the day.

"I want to go to Washington," Darnell whined. She says everything Richie does. "Come on, Mama, we never go anywhere."

"Sharon has a sky-blue LTD," Richie said, "with a tape deck."

"Lucie," I said into the phone, "thank you so much for asking, I really can't tell you how much I appreciate it, but I just have too much to contend with here. Why, there's not even a recliner in the family room. I have so much to do, and the children of course are in school."

"Well, just take them out for a couple of days." This is exactly the kind of thing you'd expect Lucie to say.

"Children need a routine," I told her, "and thank you so much for calling."

"But how are *you*?" Lucie simply refused to get off the phone. Her voice, sweet and serious, came clear as a bell across West Virginia and down through all these years. "Listen, June," she said, "you need to think of *yourself* now, you need to do something for *you*."

"Lucie," I said, "I'm just fine."

Then I hung up and went in the bathroom to vomit.

When I came out, Richie had busted one of the joysticks on the Atari and Darnell had gone to her room to cry. I looked down at the list in my hand.

Every day of my life I have made a list, and every day I do everything on it. I looked down at the list and I looked around the family room, which echoed with Atari beeps and Darnell crying. I knew I ought to go in her room and hug her but I just didn't have it in me at that time, I knew I'd start crying myself. *Pick up cleaning*, the list said. This cleaning had been at Billy's Martinizing for three weeks by then, ever since Lonnie left.

"I'll be back in a minute," I told the kids, and I went out and got in the car. We have a new car and a new house—we hadn't been in the house five months when all of this happened. "I can't stay here," Lonnie said, and then he left. He said he was real sorry. "Real sorry, ha!" I said. But I do have to say he never wanted to build the house in the first place, he wouldn't take a bit of interest. They would have put cheaper tile in the downstairs bathroom and charged us the same, for instance, if I hadn't been right there. So now the house was built and still so new that the red dirt showed in patches through the new grass all over the yard, and the patio wasn't even poured yet, just blocked out with two-by-fours, and Lonnie was over in the Colony Courts Apartments with Sharon Ledbetter, who nobody nice in this town had ever heard of, listening to rock records.

"I'll just pick up the cleaning," I said to myself, but when I got down to Billy's Martinizing, I could hardly get out of the car.

"Cleaning for Lonnie Russell," I said to the girl behind the counter. She had bright green eyelids, sitting there reading a magazine.

"Lonnie Russell," I said louder, and then she stood up and walked over and pressed the button which made all the clothes on the line go around and around.

"Ticket?" she said, and when I said "What?"—I couldn't hear her over the sound of that machine, the clothes went around and around—she said "Ticket" again.

I went through everything in my billfold, then everything in my purse. I make them, needlepoint purses, which everyone loves.

"I'm sorry," I said. "I can't find it." This was not like me to lose the ticket. I started to cry.

"Now that's all right, honey, we'll find those clothes," the girl said, looking scared, batting her bright green eyelids at me. "Don't you worry, Mrs. Russell," she said, and I guess she must have pushed a button or something because here came Billy of Billy's Martinizing himself, out of his office and over to me. You should see Billy—he is real fat and wears a blond toupee which comes right down to his eyebrows and open-neck shirts with gold chains.

"What seems to be the trouble here?" he said. He has a voice with oil in it.

"Why, just nothing at all," I said. I was crying, and the clothes went around and around, but then the girl found the cleaning and stopped the machine. It was a lot of cleaning, thirty-four dollars to be exact, and half of it Lonnie's. I saw his tan corduroy jacket and his good blue suit he bought in Charleston, all wrapped up nice in the cellophane beside my red wool dress.

"Now now," Billy said.

"Listen," I said. "My husband has left me and I am not about to pay for his cleaning."

The girl backed all the way to the office door and disappeared.

"Why, of course not," Billy said. His voice just ran all over me. "Why, I wouldn't think of such a thing," he said, and he ripped off the cellophane and started separating the clothes. He acted like all of this was exactly nothing, like it happened every day.

Lonnie's gray jacket on the right hook, my car coat on the left. I couldn't even see.

"I don't think I can stand it," I said.

"There now," said Billy, who wore a big diamond ring on his right hand. "That'll be eighteen seventy-five."

I wrote the check and crossed *Cleaning* off my list and just stood there because I had crossed off everything on my list for that day, cleaning was the last thing.

"I can't think what to do next," I said.

Billy cleared his throat. "Well, Mrs. Russell," he said, "how about a beer?"

He looked me up and down, I used to be Miss Welch High. His toupee had slid down lower over his eyes and I could see where the little hairs were stitched together in the part. "No, thanks," I finally said, but it was all I could do to get my cleaning out to the car, where I started hyperventilating like crazy the minute I got inside.

A beer! I drove home and went into Darnell's room and gave her a big, big kiss. "Get up," I said. "We're going to Pizza Hut," and when the kids got all excited I said, "and we're going to Washington too. Next weekend we're really going."

"Who's going to drive?" Richie had a point, since Lonnie always drove on trips.

I hadn't thought of that.

"I guess I am," I said, and so we went.

I'll get to the Moon Landing in a minute, but Lucie and I we go way back beyond that. After Daddy got killed in the wreck, Mama and I moved over here to Welch, West Virginia, to be near her sister—that's Lucie's mother, my Aunt Adele—since Mama had asthma, and me to raise.

"Now this is home, June," I recall Mama said when she opened the screen door. "We're going to stay here." This made me so happy. Our house was nothing much—a five-room green house with a porch that had coal dust all over it and a fat-bellied wood stove standing up like a little man in the front room, for heat. All the other houses in that holler were just like ours—they used to be company houses before the company mined out the coal and moved onto the other side of the mountain.

But I loved that house, because Mama had said we would stay there. And I loved the mountains too—they rose all around our holler, straight up and rocky and too rough for roads or settling, closing us in. Lucie hated them. But she had a nice brick house in the bottom about a mile from where we were, with a grass yard and a patio, as well as everything else I wanted in the world—a fat father with glasses who ran the Rexall drugstore and wore a red bow tie, two cute little baby brothers to play with, a cocker spaniel, air-conditioning, patent-leather shoes for Easter, a transistor radio when they first came out. Still, we were best friends. We spent all day together every day and saw every movie that came to town at least five or six times. Some of those scenes are burned forever in my mind, like the funeral in *Imitation of Life.* Lord, how we cried. We were so close in those days that sometimes I'd be thinking something and Lucie would say it out loud. I don't know what it was that turned her different unless maybe it was the heredity from her mother, my Aunt Adele.

Aunt Adele was as different from Mama as night and day. Aunt Adele taught piano and had pretensions, Lord knows where she got them. When we ate over at my house, for instance, you knew what you'd have—meat and potatoes, green beans in summer, and big red slices of the tomatoes that Mama grew in her garden right by the back door. But when we ate at Lucie's house it was no telling. You might get chicken cacciatore, for instance, or even pizza, which Lucie's family found out about when they took the trip to Myrtle Beach, or *rare* meat. The first time Aunt Adele served it to me it was a Sunday dinner and the preacher was there, I remember I felt my face go hot I was so embarrassed for her to serve something to the preacher not halfway cooked. But Uncle Earl beamed. "Darling," he said, "that's lovely," and all of us ate it like that and I never said a word. Lucie's daddy sent Aunt Adele a dozen yellow roses for her anniversary, her birthday, Christmas and Valentine's Day, any excuse you can think of. He was just crazy about Aunt Adele.

"Why couldn't Daddy have been like that?" I used to ask Mama, but she'd smile and look off down the road. Her mouth turned down when she smiled.

"Your daddy had his good points," was all she'd say.

Maybe so, but I was too young when he died to remember many of them, or even to remember him very well, since he was a traveling man and mostly always gone. We lived in eleven different towns before Mama and I moved to Welch, and I went to eight different schools all over

West Virginia. According to Daddy there was a sure thing right around the corner every time. Mama never said a word. She'd haul out the cardboard boxes which she never threw away and sometimes never even had time to unpack, and we'd put them in the car and off we'd go. We traveled light. You can't get much of anything together with a life like that. Still, Daddy was sweet. He was slight, could not have weighed more than 135, and even though he slicked his hair down careful as he could, one piece never would stay and fell forward over his eyes. He could really whistle, is the main thing I remember—he could whistle anything. He used to whistle "How Much Is That Doggie in the Window?" the year it was big, and then he'd bark. He still looked like a boy when he died, so that's how he has stayed in my mind, as a boy getting out of a car and whistling.

Anyway, Daddy's car ran off the mountain while he was working for the Jewel Tea Company door to door, and then we moved to Welch, where we stayed put and Lucie was my best friend in the world. I think the piano recital in sixth grade was the first time I caught on to any difference between us.

Now Aunt Adele's piano recitals were always a very big deal. She'd rent the banquet room of the Draper Hotel and borrow folding chairs from the funeral home. Then she'd have yellow roses in big containers standing on either side of the piano, and colored spotlights rigged up by Uncle Earl. You had to wear a semiformal and gloves. Mama always made my dress and Uncle Earl paid for the material, and of course I got the piano lessons for free too. But I didn't know that then. Ever since I found out, though, it has made a difference. That's one reason I have tried to make something of myself and Lonnie, since I realized how hard Aunt Adele and Uncle Earl tried to expose me to culture. I wanted to let them and Mama and everybody else in town know that it *took*.

I had piano lessons for the longest time and practiced a half an hour a day over at Lucie's house before I found out I was tone-deaf. But Lucie played like an angel. She wouldn't practice, either—she'd lie to her mother and say she had, but she hadn't. Still she had talent running out of her little finger—later this made me jealous. On the night of the recital when we were in fifth grade, Lucie played ahead of me, "Rustle of Spring," a flowery, runny piece, and she was so good that all the parents in the folding chairs sat absolutely still for a second before they burst into applause. Lucie curtsied, cool as a cucumber, like it was nothing at all. Aunt Adele had taught us all to curtsy.

Then it was my turn. I'll never forget it. I wore a pale blue dress with spaghetti straps and a ruffle around the bottom, and new white shoes with Cuban heels. Those were my first heels. My piece was the "Trish-Trash Polka." I could see my mama in the audience, and Uncle Earl and Aunt Adele, and everybody who was anybody in town. I started my piece. Now this was a piece with a refrain between each section and a great big finale at the end. Only, when I was almost through I realized I couldn't remember how to begin the ending. So I played the refrain again, and when that didn't work I played the part before the refrain, and then I played the refrain again. I could feel the spotlight shining hotter and hotter on my face, I could see Aunt Adele in her blue sequined evening dress lean forward in her chair. I played the refrain again. I heard somebody clear their throat and Susie Milligan, who I hated, start to giggle. I played the refrain again. I played it four more times and then I just stood up and said, "I'm sorry, I forgot my piece." Everybody clapped and clapped but they didn't fool me, I locked myself in the bathroom for the rest of the recital and wouldn't go over to Lucie's for two whole days.

We grew apart a little, after that. I quit taking piano. Lucie got interested in boys. But we still went to the movies every weekend, same as always, and sat together in church and in school, and read *Teen* magazine swinging in the swing on her front porch. The big break didn't come until 1956, I can tell you exactly because of Elvis Presley. That was the year when "Heartbreak Hotel" hit so big.

Now I had never heard of Elvis Presley until Lucie called me on the phone one day after school—it was winter— and said I had better come over there right away. "I'm busy," I said, which I was, doing I think it was math. "Come on over here anyway," Lucie said. "It's real important." So I did, and when I got there she was jumping all around the record player in the living room, saying, "June, you've just got to listen to this." Nobody else seemed to be at home right then, I remember wondering where her little brothers were. So I sat down in Uncle Earl's chair and she put one of those little red plastic rings on the record, it was a forty-five, to make it work on their record player. "Just wait," Lucie said. She held on to the edge of the record player so hard that her fingers were white and her eyes shone out from her white face in a dark liquid way I had never seen before, a way which seemed to me somehow scary. It was starting to get dark outside. She pushed a button, the forty-five dropped. Elvis came on.

I had never heard anything like it, the way his voice went way down and trembly on "I'm so lonely, baby, I'm just so lonely I could die." Elvis's voice seemed to fill up Lucie's whole darkening living room with something hot and crazy and full of pain. It made me think about things I didn't want to, such as Uncle Earl sending Aunt Adele all those roses and my own mama carrying cardboard boxes around after Daddy or just standing on the back porch and staring at nothing, which I had found her doing only a couple of days before Lucie played Elvis for me, standing on the back porch staring at an old photograph of her and Daddy they had made one time at a fair, dressed up in sailor suits. She said they rented the sailor suits from the photographer. When I came out on the porch, she put the picture in her apron pocket but I saw. "It's down at the end of Lonely Street," Elvis sang. I thought I was coming down with a virus, I stood up to go. Lucie's face shone out white in the darkness of her living room. "Don't you just love it," she said. I didn't say a thing.

I left, followed by the shaking, wanting voice of Elvis across the freezing grass. So this is how I remember it—the end of Lucie and me. Of course it wasn't truly the end, I know that, just like I know it must not have been longer than a half-hour after that when Aunt Adele came in from wherever she was, probably the grocery store, rustling her paper bags, and Uncle Earl came in from the Rexall puffing on his cigar, and the boys came back from wherever they were and started kidding Lucie about Elvis. Which they did for the next two years. I know Lucie didn't sit there in the rocking dark forever, nobody does that, the same way I know I didn't play the refrain of the "Trish-Trash Polka" over and over forever either, but still it seems like it.

Lucie got her hair cut in a pixie, painted her fingernails purple, started smoking Winston cigarettes and cutting school, and ran off in our senior year with a disc jockey named Horace Bean. She broke Uncle Earl's heart and gave Aunt Adele migraine headaches. I stayed home working part-time at the dime store and taking care of Mama, who got worse and worse. I was Miss Welch High School as I said. In the fall of my senior year I got engaged to Lonnie Russell, the quarterback.

Whole years went by after that when I didn't see Lucie although I kept up with her through Aunt Adele and Uncle Earl. Horace Bean didn't last long—Uncle

Earl had him annulled right away. Then Lucie went to college, then she taught school in Richmond and led the life of a gay divorcée. I didn't care much one way or the other. I was working two jobs to put Lonnie through school at the community college, trying to keep a decent house and take care of Mama who was living with us then. Twice while Lonnie was working for Grassy Creek Coal—this was his first job after college—they tried to send him off to other places. One time to Texas and one time to north Alabama. "Count me out!" I said. I didn't want to try to move Mama and besides I think you ought to stay in a place where people know you, and know who you are. I just couldn't see Texas, all that wind and sand, or north Alabama, or even Bluefield where Lonnie wanted to buy into a mine explosives company and would have made a lot of money I admit as it turned out, if he had. But I just couldn't see it. We stayed in Welch, and eventually Lonnie started his own mine explosives company which has done so well and I always kept the books for him. We were renting Mrs. Bradshaw's house in town and I was pregnant the summer Lucie came back and ran into Doug Young.

Ran into is exactly right! But actually he ran into us. Lucie and I were sitting out in my front yard on the lawn chairs getting some sun and trying to talk which was hard to do, our lives were so different by then, when here came a VISTA jogging up the road, sweat pouring down all over him. This was during the Poverty Program, we had

VISTAs all over the place then. And you knew it would have to be a foreigner, to run in the sun that way.

He ran right up to the gate and stopped dead in his tracks, looking at Lucie. Lucie was twenty-two or twenty-three by then, I guess, and so was I, but I had been married for years. I was as big as a house, I still have these stretch marks I got from Richie. Lucie stood up and went over to the gate to say hello and that was it. You couldn't have pried them apart with a crowbar the rest of that summer long. Aunt Adele and Uncle Earl were just beside themselves too—at last Lucie was going with somebody worth his salt, Uncle Earl said. Lonnie and I thought he was weird, though, which he was. In addition to the jogging, he used to climb the mountains *for fun*, which nobody around here has ever done. Or maybe he was just ahead of his time. Now we have all this ecology and physical fitness but nobody had it then. Lucie climbed with him. He used to spend hours testing children's eyes away up in the hollers, things like that. That stuff was part of his job. Lucie helped him. In fact she never went back to Richmond at all, just moved into his trailer on Guesses' Fork, and Uncle Earl and Aunt Adele never said a word because he had gone to Princeton.

I tried to steer clear of Lucie, she made me nervous as I said. She had this way of squinting her eyes when she looked at things, you never could tell what she thought or what she might take it into her head to do next. Such as live in a trailer with a VISTA when everyone knew it. I was so embarrassed. But Lonnie surprised me too, he said it was none of my business. I couldn't get over it—there was none of that between *us*, you can be sure, until we got married. Lonnie said I drove him crazy and especially my breasts, but I said no handling the merchandise! So it made me uneasy that summer the way they carried on.

And then the night of the Moon Landing they asked to come over to watch it on our TV, Doug naturally not having one in that trailer. It was so hot. It must have been ninety that day, and the heat never slacked off at all as night came on. I had fixed a big dinner for everybody—fried chicken and potato salad, even Lonnie would have to tell you I'm a good cook—but then after all that I got so hot I had to lay in the bathtub in the cold water for a while I felt so tired. My stomach stuck up round and white above the water where I lay, I could see the baby moving around in there. I could hear them all in the living room—Lucie and Doug and Lonnie—talking and laughing, I could hear the TV. I felt like I was miles and miles away. By the time I got out there I could see they had all had several drinks of bourbon, which Doug had brought over. Lonnie fixed me one too and I sipped along to be sociable, but it was ten o'clock before we ate and eleven o'clock before the astronauts reached the moon. Right before that, when I was in the kitchen straightening up, Lucie came in and splashed cold water all over her face. I had noticed she didn't eat much, so I asked her how she felt.

"Well," she said, "June, I might as well tell you." Lucie's eyes were dark and shining even with all the makeup washed off.

"Tell me what?" I was not so sure I wanted to know.

"I'm pregnant," Lucie said. "Me too." She looked absolutely delighted.

"Are you sure?" I asked. "Did you take a rabbit test yet?"

"No, but I'm *sure*," Lucie said. "I can just tell. Isn't it wonderful?"

"Well"—I had to sit down in a chair—"I guess it is, if you're going to get married, I mean."

Lucie looked fifteen years old with her dark hair curling around her face.

"I haven't decided," she said.

She didn't get married either, as it turned out, at least not to Doug Young. She had Tommy all by herself in Washington, then sent him home for a year for Aunt Adele to raise while she got some other degree, and then she sent for him and after a while she married the professor she's still married to now. Aunt Adele kept on teaching piano that year and hired a high school girl to look after Tommy. Aunt Adele was just fine except for the occasional migraine.

But you could have knocked me over with a feather the night of the Moon Landing when Lucie said *that*. I didn't even have time to answer because here was Lonnie at the kitchen door saying, "Come on, girls, they made it!" and grabbing me up with a big kiss so we had to go watch. *One small step for man, one large step for mankind.* It reminded me of that game Lucie and I used to play, Giant Step. It didn't seem any realer than that, them in their space suits like snowmen, walking around on the moon.

And then of course the next morning you found out that Teddy Kennedy was driving around with Mary Jo Kopechne at exactly the same time, but it was the day after that before it really hit the news. Now I wonder, did Mary Jo Kopechne think she was in love too? Anyway it seems so strange to me now that it happened that night, all of it, and all of us sitting there burning up in that rented house drinking bourbon and watching the TV news. Lonnie put a lampshade on his head and started walking around stiff-legged like a moon man, I got to giggling and Lucie did too. I laughed so hard I thought I would go into labor right then and there but I did not. We all laughed some more, and drank some more bourbon, and I can't even remember when they left.

I remember being in the bed with Lonnie though later, him and me with no sheet and the light over Dawson's Store shining in the window where I'd forgotten to pull the drapes. I got up to do it then but Lonnie said, "Leave it, I like to look at you," even as big as I was. We couldn't do anything then of course because I was too far along but I remember we went to sleep like that, me lying on my side and Lonnie's arms tight around me, him breathing through my hair into my ear, the streetlight shining white across the bed.

Lucie and I stood there looking at the Lunar Module which was a whole lot bigger than I had thought, maybe because we had watched it on that little old black-and-white TV so long ago. "Don't you remember?" Lucie said, and I said yes.

But the Lunar Module itself was so pretty in a weird kind of way—all shiny, like a combination of lace and tin-foil, like Cinderella's coach on its spidery legs. It looked magic to me right then, and I could feel my face floating up again over the crowd.

Lucie was giving advice. "You know, June," she said, "even if Lonnie is giving you plenty of money"—which he was, he's always been so generous to a fault—"the first thing you need to do now is get a job." I have always thought a woman should stay at home if humanly possible, so this went against my grain. "You need to get out, get a job," Lucie went on.

"What would I do?" I asked from my face which was floating way up there above us all.

"Well," Lucie said, looking at my needlepoint purse, "what about a craft shop or something? You always were creative."

"A craft shop!" my voice said, and then it said, "Creative!

I guess I am. I guess I'm real creative, as a matter of fact. I think I made it all up, Lucie, all of it, my marriage and Lonnie too. You remember Lonnie? Well let me tell you, I just made him up."

As soon as I said this, I knew it was true.

Lucie looked real surprised. But then she laughed, a tinkling laugh as silver as the silver on the Lunar Module before us, or maybe I mixed it all up in my head, I was mixing up the way things looked with how they sounded because my head was so far away.

"It was finished a long time ago," I said. "We were just dragging it out and Lonnie was so unhappy and I wouldn't listen or even let on that I noticed. I thought if he didn't say it, then maybe it would all go away. But it was my fault too, Lucie"—I could see this for the first time, being in Outer Space—"I tell you, I made Lonnie up."

"That's all right," Lucie said. "People do that," and then all of a sudden I forgave her being so wild and leaving Tommy that year with Aunt Adele and playing "Rustle of Spring" so well. But Lucie didn't even need it, my forgiveness. All of a sudden I knew that too.

"You'll be okay," Lucie said. *"Hey!"* She reached out to grab Tommy and Richie, who came running past like the wind. "Listen," she told them, "when this thing landed on the moon, your mom and I were right together in the same room watching it. We saw it land together, and we were both pregnant, so that means you were both in our stomachs right then, that long ago, and we were together watching. And now you're twelve years old. Isn't that amazing?" I could tell by Lucie's voice that she really did think it was amazing, just like I did.

"Huh," Tommy said. You could tell he was not impressed. Some Japanese people came up all around us and started taking pictures.

"Richie," I said, "isn't that something?" but Richie grinned just like Tommy and said, "So what?"

Tongues of Fire

The year I was thirteen—1957—my father had a nervous breakdown, my brother had a wreck, and I started speaking in tongues. The nervous breakdown had been going on for a long time before I knew anything about it. Then one day that fall, Mama took me downtown in the car to get some Baskin-Robbins ice cream, something she never did, and while we were sitting on the curly chairs facing each other across the little white table, Mama took a deep breath, licked her red lipstick, leaned forward in a very significant way, and said, "Karen, you may have noticed that your father is *not himself* lately."

Not himself! Who was he, then? What did she mean? But I had that feeling you get in your stomach when something really important happens. I knew this was a big deal.

Mama looked all around, as if for spies. She waited until

the ice cream man went through the swinging pink doors, into the back of his shop.

"Karen," she said, so low I could hardly hear her, "your father is having a nervous breakdown."

"He is?" I said stupidly.

The ice cream man came back.

"Sssh," Mama said. She caught my eye and nodded gravely, once. "Don't eat that ice cream so fast, honey," she said a minute later. "It'll give you a headache."

And this was the only time she ever mentioned my father's nervous breakdown out loud, in her whole life. The older kids already knew, it turned out. Everybody had wanted to keep it from me, the baby. But then the family doctor said Mama *ought* to tell me, so she did. But she did not elaborate, then or ever, and in retrospect I am really surprised that she ever told me at all. Mama grew up in Birmingham, so she talked in a very Southern voice and wore spectator heels and linen dresses that buttoned up the front and required a great deal of ironing by Missie, the maid. Mama's name was Dee Rose. She said that when she married Daddy and came up here to the wilds of north Alabama to live, it was like moving to Siberia. It was like moving to Outer Mongolia, she said. Mama's two specialties were Rising to the Occasion and Rising Above It All, whatever "it" happened to be. Mama believed that if you can't say something nice, say nothing at all. If you don't discuss something, it doesn't exist. This is the way our family handled all of its problems, such as my father's quarrel with my Uncle Dick or my sister's promiscuity or my brother's drinking.

Mama had long red fingernails and shiny yellow hair which she wore in a bubble cut. She looked like a movie star. Mama drank a lot of gin and tonics and sometimes she would start on them early, before five o'clock. She'd wink at Daddy and say, "Pour me one, honey, it's already dark underneath the house." Still, Mama had very rigid ideas, as I was to learn, about many things. Her ideas about nervous breakdowns were:

1. *The husband* should not *have a nervous breakdown.*
2. *Nobody can mention the nervous breakdown. It is shameful.*
3. *The children must* behave *at all times during the nervous breakdown.*
4. *The family must keep up appearances at all costs.* Nobody should know.

Mama and I finished our ice cream and she drove us home in the white Cadillac, and as soon as we got there I went up in my treehouse to think about Daddy's breakdown. I knew it was true. *So this is it,* I thought. This had been it all along. This explained the way my father's eye twitched and watered now, behind his gold-rimmed glasses. My father's eyes were deep-set and sort of mournful at best, even before the twitch. They were an odd, arresting shade of very pale blue which I have never seen since, except in my sister, Ashley. Ashley was beautiful, and my father was considered to be very good-looking, I knew that, yet he had always been too slow-moving and thoughtful for me. I would have preferred a more military model, a snappy go-getter of a dad. My dad looked like a professor at the college, which he was not. Instead he ran a printing company with my Uncle Dick, until their quarrel. Now he ran it by himself—or rather his secretary, Mrs. Eunice Merriman, ran it mostly by herself during the time he had his nervous breakdown. Mrs. Eunice Merriman was a large, imposing woman with her pale blond hair swept up in a beehive hairdo as smooth and hard as a helmet. She wore glasses with harlequin frames. Mrs. Merriman reminded me of some warlike figure from Norse mythology. She was not truly fierce, however, except in her devotion to my father, who spent more and more time lying on the daybed upstairs in his study, holding books or magazines in his hands but not reading them, looking out the bay window, at the mountains across the river. What was he thinking about?

"Oh *honestly*, Karen!" my mother exploded when I asked her this question. My mother was much more interested, on the day I asked her, in the more immediate question of whether or not I had been invited to join the Sub-Deb Club. The answer was yes.

But there was no answer to the question of what my

father might be thinking about. I knew that he had wanted
to be a writer in his youth. I knew that he had been the
protégé of some old poet or other down at the university
in Tuscaloosa, that he had written a novel which was never
published, that he had gone to the Pacific Theater in the
War. I had always imagined the Pacific Theater as a literal
theater, somewhat like the ornate Rialto in Birmingham
with its organ that rose up and down mechanically from
the orchestra pit, its gold-leaf balconies, its chandelier as
big as a Chevrolet. In this theater, my father might have
watched such movies as *Sands of Iwo Jima* or *To Hell and
Back*. Now it occurred to me, for the first time, that he
might have witnessed horrors. Horrors! Sara Nell Buie, at
school, swore that *her* father had five Japanese ears in a
cigar box from the Philippines. Perhaps my father had seen
horrors too great to be borne. Perhaps he too had ears.

But this did not seem likely, to look at him. It seemed
more like mononucleosis to me. He was just *lying on the
daybed*. Now he'd gotten his days and nights turned around
so that he had to take sleeping tablets; he went to the printing company for only an hour or two each day. He rallied
briefly at gin-and-tonic time, but his conversation tended
to lapse in the middle of itself during dinner, and frequently he left the table early. My mother rose above
these occasions in the way she had been trained to do as a
girl in Birmingham, in the way she was training Ashley
and me to do: She talked incessantly, about anything

that entered her head, to fill the void. This was another of Mama's rules:

A lady never lets a silence fall.

Perhaps the most exact analysis of my father's nervous breakdown was provided by Missie, one day when I was up in the treehouse and she was hanging out laundry on the line almost directly below me, talking to the Gardeners' maid from next door. "You mean Missa Graffenreid?" Missie said. "He have *lost his starch*, is all. He be getting it back directly."

In the meantime, Mama seemed to grow in her vivacity, in her busyness, taking up the slack. Luckily my sister, Ashley, was a senior at Lorton Hall that year, so this necessitated a lot of conferences and visits to colleges. The guidance counselor at Lorton Hall wanted Ashley to go to Bryn Mawr, up North, but after the visit to Bryn Mawr my mother returned with her lips pressed tight together in a little red bow. "Those girls were *not ladies*," she reported to us all, and Bryn Mawr was never mentioned again except by Ashley, later, in fits of anger at the way her life turned out. The choices narrowed to Converse College in Spartanburg, South Carolina; Meredith College in Raleigh, North Carolina; Sophie Newcomb in New Orleans; and Sweet Briar, in Virginia. My mama was dead set on Sweet Briar.

So Mama and Ashley were very busy with college visits

and with all the other activities of Ashley's senior year at Lorton Hall. There were countless dresses to buy, parties to give and go to. I remember one Saturday that fall when Ashley had a Coke party in the back garden, for the senior girls and their mothers. Cokes and finger sandwiches were served. Missie had made the finger sandwiches the day before and put them on big silver trays, covered by damp tea towels. I watched the party from the window of my room upstairs, which gave me a terrific view of the back garden and the red and yellow fall leaves and flowers, and the girls and their mothers like chrysanthemums themselves. I watched them from my window—just as my father watched them, I suppose, from his.

My mother loved to shop, serve on committees, go to club meetings, and entertain. (Probably she should have been running Graffenreid Printing Co. all along—I see this now—but of course such an idea would not have entered anyone's head at the time.) Mama ran the Flower Guild of the Methodist church, which we attended every Sunday morning, minus my father. She was the recording secretary of the Ladies' Auxiliary, which literally *ran the town* as far as I could see; she was a staunch member of the Garden Club and the Bluebird Book Club.

Her bridge club met every Thursday at noon for lunch and bridge, rotating houses. This bridge club went on for years and years beyond my childhood, until its members began to die or move to Florida. It fascinated me. I loved those summer Thursdays when I was out of school and the bridge club came to our house—the fresh flowers, the silver, the pink cloths on the bridge tables which were set up for the occasion in the Florida room, the way Mama's dressing room smelled as she dressed, that wonderful mixture of loose powder (she used a big lavender puff) and cigarette smoke (Salems) and Chanel No. 5. The whole bridge club dressed to the hilt. They wore hats, patent-leather shoes, and dresses of silk shantung. The food my mama and Missie gave them was wonderful—is still, to this day, my very idea of elegance, even though it is not a menu I'd ever duplicate; and it was clear to me, even then, that the way these ladies were was a way I'd never be.

But on those Thursdays, I'd sit at the top of the stairs, peering through the banisters into the Florida room, where they lunched in impossible elegance, and I got to eat everything they did, from my own plate which Missie had fixed specially for me: a pink molded salad that melted on the tongue, asparagus-cheese soufflé, and something called Chicken Crunch that involved mushroom soup, chicken, Chinese noodles, pecans, and Lord knows what else. All of Mama's bridge-lunch recipes required gelatin or mushroom soup or pecans. This was Lady Food.

So—it was the year that Mama was lunching, Daddy was lying on the daybed, and Ashley was Being a Senior. My brother, Paul, had already gone away to college, to Washington and Lee up in Virginia. At that time in my life, I knew Paul only by sight. He was incredibly old. Nice, but very old and very busy, riding around in cars full of other boys, dashing off here and there when he was home, which was seldom. He used to tell me knock-knock jokes, and come up behind me and buckle my knees. I thought Paul's degree of bustle and zip was *promising*, though. I certainly hoped he would be more active than Daddy. But who could tell? I rarely saw him.

I rarely saw *anybody* in my family, or so I felt. I floated through it all like a dandelion puff on the air, like a wisp of smoke, a ghost. During the year of my father's nervous breakdown, I became invisible in my family. But I should admit that even before my invisibility I was scarcely noticeable, a thin girl, slight, brown-haired and brown-eyed, *undeveloped* (as Mrs. Black put it delicately in health class). There was no sign of a breast anyplace on my chest even though some other girls my age wore B and even C cups, I saw them in gym. I had gone down to Sears on the bus by myself the previous summer and bought myself two training bras, just so I'd have them, but my mother had never mentioned this subject to me at all, of course. And even after I got the training bras, I remained—I felt—still ugly, and still invisible in the midst of my gorgeous family.

Perhaps it is not surprising that I turned to God.

I had always been *interested* in religion, anyway. When I was a little girl, my favorite part of the summer was Vacation Bible School, with the red Kool-Aid in the little Dixie cups and the Lorna Doone cookies at break. I loved to color in the twelve disciples. I loved to make lanyards. I loved to sing "You Are My Sunshine" and "Red and Yellow, Black and White, They Are Precious in His Sight." I loved to hold hands with Alice Field, who was my best friend for years and years until her family moved to Little Rock, Arkansas. I loved Mrs. Treble Roach, the teacher of Vacation Bible School, a plump soft woman like a beanbag chair, who hugged us all the time. Mrs. Treble Roach gave us gold stars when we were good, and I was *very* good. I got hundreds of gold stars over the years and I believe I still have them upstairs someplace in a jewelry box, like ears.

I had always liked church too, although it was less fun. I associated church with my grandparents, since we sat with them every Sunday, third pew from the back on the left-hand side of the little stone Methodist church which my grandfather had attended all his life, which my grandmother had attended since their marriage fifty years before. Usually my mother went to church too; sometimes Ashley went to church, under duress ever since she became an atheist in tenth grade, influenced by an English teacher who was clearly *not a lady*; my father attended only on Easter. Frankly, I liked those Sundays when none of them made it, when Mama just dropped me off in front of the church and I went in all alone, clutching my quarter for the collection plate, to sit with my grandparents. Even though I was invisible in my own family, my grandparents noticed me plenty. I was their good, good little girl . . . certainly, I felt, their favorite. I did everything I could to ensure that this was true.

My grandmother had wispy blue hair and a whole lot of earrings and brooches that matched. She was the author of four books of poems which Daddy had printed up for her at the printing company. She suffered from colitis, and was ill a lot. One thing you never wanted to do with Grandmother was ask her how she felt—she'd *tell* you, gross details you didn't want to know. My mama, of course, was entirely above this kind of thing, never referring to her own or anybody else's body in any way. My grandfather wore navy-blue suits to church with red suspenders underneath. He was a boxy little man who ran the bus station and had a watch that could tell you the time in Paris, London, and Tokyo. I coveted this watch and had already asked Grandaddy to leave it to me when he died, a request that seemed to startle him.

After church, I'd walk up the street with my grandparents to their house on the corner across from the Baptist church and eat lunch, which frequently ended with lemon meringue pie, my favorite. I kept a close eye out the window for Baptists, whose service was dismissed half an hour later than ours. There were so many Baptists that it took them longer to do everything. In pretty weather, I sat out on the front porch so that I could see the Baptists more clearly. They wore loud suits, and made more noise in general than the quiet Methodists.

Our church had only forty-two members and about twenty of them, like my grandparents, were so old as to be almost dead already. I was not even looking forward to joining the MYF, which I'd be eligible for next year, because it had only eight members, two of them definite nerds. All they did was collect food for the poor at Thanksgiving, and stuff like that. The BTU, on the other hand, did great stuff such as have progressive dinners, Sweetheart Banquets, and go on trips to Gulf Shores. The BTU was a much snappier outfit than the MYF, but I knew better than to ask to join it. My mother had already explained to me the social ranking of the churches: Methodist at the top, attended by doctors and lawyers and other "nice" families; Presbyterian slightly down the scale, attended by store owners; then the vigorous Baptists; then the Church of Christ, who thought they were the only real church in town and said so. They said everybody else in town was going to hell except for them. They had hundreds of members. And then, of course, at the *very bottom* of the church scale were those little churches out in the surrounding county, some of them recognizable denominations (Primitive Baptist) and some of them not (Church of the Nazarene, Tar River Holiness) where people were reputed to yell out, fall down in fits, and throw their babies. I didn't know what this *meant*, exactly, but I knew I'd love to see it, for it promised drama far beyond the dull responsive readings of the Methodists and their rote mumbling of the Nicene Creed.

Anyway, I had been sitting on my grandparents' front porch for years eating pie and envying the Baptists, waiting without much hope to be seized by God for His heavenly purpose, bent to His will, as in *God's Girl*, my favorite book—a biography of Joan of Arc.

So far, nothing doing.

But then, that fall of Daddy's nervous breakdown, the Methodist church was visited by an unusually charismatic young preacher named Johnny Rock Malone while Mr. Treble Roach, our own preacher, was down at Duke having a hernia operation. I was late to church that day and arrived all by myself, after the service had already started. The congregation was on its feet singing "I Come to the Garden Alone," one of my favorite hymns. One unfamiliar voice led all the rest. I slipped in next to Grandaddy, found the right page in the hymnal, and craned my neck around Miss Eulalie Butters's big black hat to see who was up there singing so nice. It looked like an angel to me—probably the angel Gabriel, because of his curly blond hair. And he was so *young*—just out of seminary, somebody said after the service. It was a warm fall Sunday, and rays of colored light shot through the stained-glass windows at the side of the church to glance off Johnny Rock Malone's pale face. "He *walks* with me, and He *talks* with me," we sang. My heart started beating double time. Johnny Rock Malone stretched out his long thin arms and spread his long white fingers. "Beloved," he said, curling his fingers, "let us pray."

But I never closed my eyes that day, staring instead at the play of light on Johnny Rock Malone's fair face. It was almost like a kaleidoscope. Then the round rosy window behind him, behind the altar, began to *pulse* with light, to glow with light, now brighter now not, like a neon sign. I got the message. I was no dummy. In a way, I had been waiting all my life for this to happen.

The most notable thing about me as a child—before I got religious, I mean—was my obsessive reading. I had always been an inveterate reader of the sort who hides underneath the covers with a flashlight and reads *all night long*. But I did not read casually, or for mere entertainment, or for information. What I wanted was to feel all wild and trembly inside, an effect first produced by *The Secret Garden*, which I'd read maybe twenty times. And the Rev. Johnny Rock Malone looked exactly the way I had always pictured Colin! In fact, listening to him preach, I felt exactly the way I felt when I read *The Secret Garden*, just exactly.

Other books which had affected me strongly were *Little Women*, especially the part where Beth dies, and *Gone With the Wind*, especially the part where Melanie dies. I had long hoped for a wasting disease, such as leukemia, to test my mettle. I also loved *Marjorie Morningstar, A Tree Grows in Brooklyn, Heidi*, and books like *Dear and Glorious Physician, The Shoes of the Fisherman, Christy*, and anything at all about horses and saints. I had read all the Black Stallion books, of course, as well as all the Marguerite Henry books.

But my all-time favorite was *God's Girl,* especially the frontispiece illustration picturing Joan as she knelt and "prayed without ceasing for guidance from God," whose face was depicted overhead, in a thunderstorm. Not only did I love Joan of Arc, I wanted to *be* her.

The only man I had ever loved more than Colin of *The Secret Garden,* to date, was Johnny Tremain, from Esther Forbes's book of that title. I used to wish that it was *me*—not Johnny Tremain—who'd had the hot silver spilled on my hand. I would have suffered anything (everything) for Johnny Tremain.

But on that fateful Sunday morning, Johnny Rock Malone eclipsed both Colin and Johnny Tremain in my affections. It was a wipeout. I felt as fluttery and wild as could be. In fact I felt too crazy to pay attention to the sermon which Johnny Rock Malone was, by then, almost finished with. I tried to concentrate, but my mind was whirling. The colors from the windows seemed to deepen and swirl. And then, suddenly, I heard him loud and clear, reading from Revelations: "And I saw a great white throne, and Him that sat on it, from whose face the earth and heaven fled away; and there was found no place for them. And I saw the dead, small and great, stand before God, and the books were opened . . . and whosoever was not found written in the book of life was cast into the lake of fire."

I can't remember much about what happened after that. I got to shake hands with him as we left the church, and I was surprised to find that his hand was cool, not burning hot—and, though bony, somehow as soft as a girl's. I looked hard at Johnny Rock Malone as he stood in front of our pretty little church, shaking hands. He was on his way to someplace else, over in Mississippi. We would never see him again. *I* would never see him again. And yet somehow I felt exhilarated and *satisfied*, in a way. I can't explain it. Back at my grandparents' house, I couldn't even eat any lemon meringue pie. I felt shaky and hot, like I might be getting a virus. I went home early.

My father was upstairs in his study, door closed. Nobody else was home. I wandered the house. Then I sat in the Florida room for a while, staring out at the day. After a while, I picked up my mother's sewing basket from the coffee table, got a needle and threaded it with blue thread, and sewed all the fingers of my left hand together, through the cuticle. Then I held out my hand and admired it, wishing desperately for my best friend Alice Field, of Little Rock. I had no best friend now, nobody to show my amazing hand to. Weird little Edwin Lee lived right across the street, but it was inconceivable that I would show *him*, the nerd, such a hand as this. So I showed it to nobody. I left it sewed up until Mama's white Cadillac pulled in the driveway, and then I cut the thread between my fingers and pulled it all out.

It was about this time too that I began to pray a lot (*without ceasing* was my intention) and set little fires all around the neighborhood. These fires were nothing much.

I'd usually take some shredded newspapers or some Kleenex, find a few sticks, and they'd burn themselves out in a matter of minutes. I made a fire in my treehouse, in our garage, in the sink, in the basement, on Mrs. Butters's back patio, on Mr. and Mrs. Harold Castle's front porch, and in little Charlotte Lee's playhouse. Here I went too far, singeing off the hair of her Barbie doll. She never could figure out how it happened.

I entertained visions of being a girl evangelist, of appearing with Billy Graham on television, of traveling throughout Mississippi with Johnny Rock Malone. I'd be followed everywhere I went by a little band of my faithful. I made a small fire in the bed of Ashley's new boyfriend's pickup truck while he and my sister were in the den petting and watching the Hit Parade. They didn't have any idea that I was outside in the night, watching them through the window, making a fire in the truck. They all thought I was in bed!

Although I was praying a lot, my prayers were usually specific, as opposed to *without ceasing*. For instance I'd tell one friend I'd go shopping with her, and then something I really wanted to do would come up, and I'd call back and say I couldn't come after all, that my grandmother had died, and then I would go to my room and fling myself to the floor and pray without ceasing that my lie would not be found out, and that my grandmother would not really die. I made big deals with God—*if* He would make sure I got away with it this time, I would talk to Edwin Lee for five minutes on the bus, three days in a row, or I would clean out my closet. He did His part; I did mine. I grew in power every day.

I remember so well that important Friday when I was supposed to spend the night with Margaret Applewhite. Now Margaret Applewhite was totally boring, in my opinion—my only rival in the annual spelling bee (she won in third, I won in fourth and fifth, she beat me out in sixth with *catarrh*, which still rankled). Margaret Applewhite wore a training bra too. Our mothers, who played bridge together, encouraged our friendship. I'd rather do just about *anything*, even watch Kate Smith on TV, than spend time with boring Margaret Applewhite. Still, earlier that week when she'd called and invited me, I couldn't for the life of me think of any good reason to say no, so I'd said yes. Then that Friday right before sixth period, Tammy Lester came up to my locker popping her gum (against the rules: We were not allowed to chew gum in school) and— wonder of wonders—asked me to come home with her after school that very day and spend the night.

Tammy Lester! Shunned by Sub-Debs, sent to Detention, noticed by older boys. I couldn't believe it. I admired Tammy Lester more than any other girl in my entire class, I'd watched her from afar the way I had watched the Baptists. Tammy Lester lived out in the county someplace (in a trailer, it was rumored), she was driven in to school each morning by one or the other of her wild older brothers in a red pickup truck (these brothers slicked back their hair with grease, they wore their cigarette packs rolled up in the sleeves of their T-shirts), and best of all, she was missing a tooth right in front, and nobody had taken her to the dentist yet to get it fixed. The missing tooth gave Tammy a devilish, jaunty look. Also, as I would learn later, she could whistle through this hole, and spit twenty feet.

Her invitation was offhand. "You wanna come home with me today?" she asked, in a manner that implied she didn't give a hoot whether I did or not. "Buddy's got to come into town tomorrow morning anyway, so he could bring you back."

"All right," I said, trying to sound casual.

"I'll meet you out front when the bell rings." Tammy flashed me her quick dark grin. She popped her gum, and was gone.

I didn't hesitate for a minute. I stopped Margaret Applewhite on her way to health class. "Listen," I said in a rush, "I'm so sorry I can't come spend the night with you, but my mother is having an emergency hysterectomy today, so I have to go straight home and help out." I had just learned about hysterectomies, from a medical book in the library.

Margaret's boring brown eyes widened. "Is she going to be all right?"

I sucked in my breath dramatically and looked brave. "We hope so," I said. "They think they can get it all."

Margaret walked into health. I sank back against the mustard-yellow tile walls as, suddenly, it hit me: Margaret's mother knew my mother! What if Margaret's mother called my mother, and Mama found out? She'd be furious, not only because of the lie but because of the nature of the lie—Mama would *die* before she'd ever mention something like a hysterectomy. Mama referred to everything below the belt as "down there," an area she dealt with darkly, indirectly, and only when necessary. "Trixie Vopel is in the hospital for tests," she might say. "She's been having trouble *down there.*" *Down there* was a foreign country, like Africa or Nicaragua.

What to do? I wrote myself an excuse from gym, signed my mother's name, turned it in and then went to the infirmary, where I lay down on a hard white cot and prayed without ceasing for upwards of an hour. I promised a lot: If Mama did not find out, I would sit with Lurice May at lunch on Monday (a dirty fat girl who kept her head wrapped up in a scarf and was rumored to have lice), I would be nice to Edwin Lee three times for fifteen minutes each, I would clean out under my bed, I would give back the perfume and the ankle bracelet I had stolen from Ashley, and I would put two dollars of my saved-up babysitting money in the collection plate at church on Sunday. It was the best I could do. Then I called my mother from the infirmary phone, and to my surprise, she said, "Oh, of course," in a distracted way when I asked if I could spend the night with Tammy Lester. She did not even ask what Tammy's father did.

Then *"Karen,"* she said in a pointed way that meant this was what she was *really* interested in, "do you have any idea where your sister is right now?"

"What?" I couldn't even remember *who* my sister was, right now.

"Ashley," Mama said. "The school called and asked if she was sick. Apparently she just never showed up at school today."

"I'll bet they had some secret senior thing," I said.

"Oh." Mama sounded relieved. "Well, maybe so. Now who is it you're spending the night with?" she asked again, and I told her. "And what did you say her father does?"

"Lawyer," I said.

Spending the night with Tammy Lester was the high point of my whole life up to that time. She did *not* live in a trailer, as rumored, but in an old unpainted farmhouse with two boarded-up windows, settled unevenly onto cinder-block footings. A mangy dog lay up under the house. Chickens roamed the property. The porch sagged. Wispy ancient curtains blew out eerily at the upstairs windows. The whole yard was strewn with parts of things—cars, stoves, bedsprings, unimaginable machine parts rusting among the weeds. I loved it. Tammy led me everywhere and showed me everything: her secret place, a tent of willows, down by the creek; the grave of her favorite dog, Buster, and the collar he had worn; an old chicken house that her brothers had helped her make into a playhouse; a haunted shack down the road; the old Packard out back that you could get in and pretend you were taking a trip. "Now we're in Nevada," Tammy said, shifting gears. "Now we're in the Grand Canyon. Now we're in the middle of the desert. It's hot as hell out here, ain't it?"

I agreed.

At suppertime, Tammy and I sat on folding chairs pulled up to the slick oilcloth-covered table beneath a bare hanging light bulb. Her brothers had disappeared. Tammy seemed to be cooking our supper; she was heating up Dinty Moore stew straight out of the can.

"Where's your daddy?" I asked.

"Oh, he's out West on a pipeline," she said, vastly unconcerned.

"Where's your mama?" I said. I had seen her come in from work earlier that afternoon, a pudgy, pale redheaded woman who drove a light blue car that looked like it would soon join the others in the backyard.

"I reckon she's reading her Bible," Tammy said, as if this were a perfectly ordinary thing to be doing on a Friday night at gin-and-tonic time. "She'll eat after while."

Tammy put half of the Dinty Moore stew into a chipped red bowl and gave it to me. It was delicious, lots better than Lady Food. She ate hers right out of the saucepan. "Want to split a beer?" she said, and I said sure, and she got us one—a Pabst Blue Ribbon—out of the icebox. Of course I had never tasted beer before. But I thought it was great.

That night, I told Tammy about my father's nervous breakdown, and she told me that her oldest brother had gone to jail for stealing an outboard motor. She also told me about the lady down the road who had chopped off her husband's hands with an ax while he was "laying up drunk." I told her that I was pretty sure God had singled me out for a purpose which he had not yet revealed, and Tammy nodded and said her mother had been singled out too. I sat right up in bed. "What do you mean?" I asked.

"Well, she's real religious," Tammy said, "which is why she don't get along with Daddy too good." I nodded. I had already figured out that Daddy must be the dark handsome one that all the children took after. "And she was a preacher's daughter too, see, so she's been doing it all her life."

"Doing what?" I asked into the dark.

"Oh, talking in tongues of fire," Tammy said matter-of-factly, and a total thrill crept over me, the way I had always wanted to feel. I had hit pay dirt at last.

"I used to get embarrassed, but now I don't pay her much mind," Tammy said.

"Listen," I said sincerely. "I would give *anything* to have a mother like that."

Tammy whistled derisively through the hole in her teeth.

But eventually, because I was already so good at collective

bargaining, we struck a deal: I would get to go to church with Tammy and her mother, the very next Sunday if possible, and in return, I would take Tammy to the country club. (I could take her when Mama wasn't there; I was allowed to sign for things.) Tammy and I stayed up talking nearly all night long. She was even more fascinating than I'd thought. She had breasts, she knew how to drive a car, and she was part Cherokee. Toward morning, we cut our fingers with a kitchen knife and swore to be best friends forever.

The next day, her brother Mike drove me into town at about one o'clock. He had to see a man about a car. He smoked cigarettes all the way, and scowled at everything. He didn't say a word to me. I thought he was wonderful.

I arrived home just in time to intercept the delivery boy from the florist's. "I'll take those in," I said, and pinched the card which said, "For Dee Rose. Get well soon. Best wishes from Lydia and Lou Applewhite." I left the flowers on the doorstep, where they would create a little mystery later on, when Mama found them, and went upstairs to my room and prayed without ceasing, a prayer of thanksgiving for the special favors I felt He had granted me lately. Then before long I fell asleep, even as a huge argument raged all over the house, upstairs and down, between Mama and my sister, Ashley who had *just come in*, having stayed out all day and all night long.

"If a girl loses her reputation, she has lost *everything*," Mama said. "She has lost her Most Precious Possession."

"So what? So what?" Ashley screamed. "All you care about is appearances. Who cares what I do, in this screwed-up family? Who really cares?"

It went on and on, while I melted down and down into my pink piqué comforter, hearing them but not really hearing them, dreaming instead of the lumpy sour bed out at Tammy's farm, of the moonlight on the wispy graying curtains at her window, of a life so hard and flinty that it might erupt at any moment into tongues of fire.

N ot only was the fight over with by Sunday morning, but it was so far over with as not to have happened at all. I came in the kitchen late, to find Mama and Ashley still in their bathrobes, eating sticky buns and reading the funnies. It looked like nobody would be available to drive me to church. Clearly, both Ashley and Mama had Risen Above It All—Mama, to the extent that she was virtually levitating as the day wore on, hovering a few feet off the floor in her Sunday seersucker suit as she exhorted us all to hurry, hurry, hurry. Our reservations were for one o'clock. The whole family was going out for brunch at the country club.

Daddy was going too.

I still wonder what she said to him to get him up and dressed and out of there. I know it was the kind of thing that meant a lot to her—a public act, an event that meant

See, here is our whole happy family out together at the country club; see, we are a perfectly normal family; see, there is nothing wrong with us at all. And I know that Daddy loved her.

Our table overlooked the first tee of the golf course. Our waiter, Louis, had known Daddy ever since he was a child. Daddy ordered a martini. Mama ordered a gin and tonic. Ashley ordered a lemon Coke. I ordered lemonade. Mama was so vivacious that she almost gave off light. Her eyes sparkled, her hair shone, her red lipstick glistened. She and Ashley were discussing which schools her fellow seniors hoped to attend, and why. Ashley was very animated too. Watching them, I suddenly realized how much Ashley was like Mama. Ashley laughed and gestured with her pretty hands. I watched her carefully. I knew Mama thought Ashley had lost her Most Precious Possession (things were different *down there*), yet she didn't look any different to me. She wore a hot-pink sheath dress and pearls. She looked terrific.

I turned my attention to Daddy, curiously, because I felt all of a sudden that I had not really seen him for years and years. He might as well have been off on a pipeline, as far as I was concerned. Our drinks arrived, and Daddy sipped at his martini. He perked up. He looked weird, though. His eyes were sunken in his head, like the limestone caves above the Tombigbee River. His skin was as white and dry as a piece of Mama's stationery. My father bought all his clothes in New York so they were always quite elegant, but now they hung on him like on a coat rack. How much weight had he lost? Twenty pounds? Thirty? We ordered lunch. Daddy ordered another martini.

Now he was getting entirely too perky, he moved his hands too much as he explained to Ashley the theory behind some battle in some war. He stopped talking only long enough to stand up and shake hands with the friends who came by our table to speak to him, friends who had not seen him for months and months. He didn't touch his food. Underneath my navy-blue dress with the sailor collar, I was sweating, in spite of my mother's pronouncement:

Horses sweat, men perspire, and women glow.

I could feel it trickling down my sides. I wondered if, as I grew up, this would become an uncontrollable problem, whether I would have to wear dress shields. We all ordered baked Alaska, the chef's speciality, for dessert. My mother smiled and smiled. I was invisible. When the baked Alaska arrived, borne proudly to our table by Louis, nobody could put out the flames. Louis blew and blew. Other waiters ran over, beating at it with linen napkins. My mother laughed merrily. "For goodness' sakes!" she said. My daddy looked stricken. Finally they got it out and we all ate some, except for Daddy.

Gazing past my family to the golfers out on the grass beyond us, I had a sudden inspiration. I knew what to do. I emerged from invisibility long enough to say, "Hey, Daddy, let's go out and putt," and he put his napkin promptly on the table and stood right up. "Sure thing, honey," he said, sounding for all the world like my own daddy. He smiled at me. I took his hand, remembering then who I had been before the nervous breakdown: Daddy's little girl. We went down the stairs, past the snack bar, and out to the putting green at the side of the building.

My dad was a good golfer. I was not bad myself. We shared a putter from the Pro Shop. We started off and soon it was clear that we were having a great time, that this was a good idea. The country club loomed massively behind us. The emerald grass, clipped and even, stretched out on three sides in front of us, as far as we could see, ending finally in a stand of trees here, a rolling hill there. This expanse of grass, dotted with pastel golfers, was both comforting and exhilarating. It was a nine-hole putting green. On the seventh hole, we were tied, if you figured in the handicap that my father had given himself. I went first, overshooting on my second stroke, sinking it with a really long shot on my third. I looked back over at Daddy to make sure he had seen my putt, but clearly he had not. He was staring out over the grass toward the horizon, beyond the hill.

"Your turn!" I called out briskly, tossing him the putter.

What happened next was awful.

In one terrible second, my father turned to me, face slack, mouth agape, then fell to his knees on the putting green, cowering, hands over his face. The putter landed on

the grass beside him. He was crying. I didn't know what
to do. I just stood there, and then suddenly the putting
green was full of people—the pro, Bob White, in his jacket
with his name on it, helping Daddy to his feet; our dentist,
Dr. Reap, holding him by the other elbow as they walked
him to our white Cadillac which Mama had driven around
to pick us up in. Ashley cried all the way home. So did
Daddy.

It was not until that day that I realized that the nervous
breakdown was real, that Daddy was really sick.

I ran upstairs and prayed without ceasing for a solid
hour, by the clock, that Daddy would get well and that we
would all be *all right*, for I had come to realize somehow,
during the course of that afternoon, that we might *not* be.
We might never be all right again.

A t least I had a New Best Friend. I banished all memory
of Alice Field, without remorse. Tammy Lester and
I became, for the rest of that spring, inseparable. The first
time I brought her to my house, I did it without asking. I
didn't want to give Mama a chance to say no. And although
we had not discussed it, Tammy showed up dressed more
like a town girl than I had ever seen her—a plaid skirt, a
white blouse, loafers, her dark hair pulled back and up into
a cheerful ponytail. She could have been a cheerleader. She
could have been a member of the Sub-Deb Club. No one

could have ever guessed what she had in her pocket—a pack of Kents and a stolen kidney stone once removed from her neighbor, Mrs. Gillespie, who had kept it in a jar on her mantel. But even though Tammy looked so nice, Mama was giving her the third degree. "How many brothers and sisters did you say you had?" and "Where was your mama *from?*"

This interrogation took place upstairs in Mama's dressing room. Suddenly, to everyone's surprise, Daddy lurched in to fill the doorway and say, "Leave those little girls alone, Dee Rose, you've got your hands full already," and oddly enough, Mama *did* leave us alone then. She didn't say another word about it at the time, turning back to her nails, or even later, as spring progressed and Ashley's increasing absences and moodiness became more of a problem. Before long, Daddy refused to join us even for dinner. Mama *did* have her hands full. If I could occupy myself, so much the better.

I will never forget the first time I was allowed to go to church with Tammy and her mother. I had spent the night out at the farm, and in the morning I was awake long before it was time to leave. I dressed carefully, in the yellow dress and jacket Mama had ordered for me only a couple of months before from Rich's in Atlanta. It was already getting too small. Tammy and her mother both looked at my outfit with some astonishment. They didn't have any particular church clothes, it turned out. At least, they didn't have any church clothes as fancy as these. Tammy wore a black dress which was much too old for her, clearly a hand-me-down from someplace, and her mother wore the same formless slacks and untucked shirt she always wore. I could never tell any of her clothes apart. For breakfast that morning, we had Hi-Ho cakes, which we ate directly from their cellophane wrappers, and Dr Peppers. Then we went out and got into their old blue car, which threatened not to start. *Oh no!* I found myself suddenly, terribly upset. I realized then how very much I was dying to hear Tammy's mother speak in tongues of fire, a notion that intrigued me more and more the better I got to know her, because usually she *didn't speak at all.* Never! Her pale gray eyes were fixed on distance, the way my daddy's had been that day at the golf course. The engine coughed and spluttered, died. Then finally Tammy's mother suggested that Tammy and I should push her down the muddy rutted driveway and she'd pop the clutch. I had never heard of such a thing. In my family, a man in a uniform, from a garage, came to start cars that wouldn't start. Still, we pushed. It started. I got mud all over the bottom of my yellow dress.

Which didn't matter at all, I saw as soon as we got to the church. There were old men in overalls, younger men in coveralls with their names stitched on their pockets, girls in jeans, boys in jeans. The men stood around by their trucks in the parking lot, smoking cigarettes. The women went on in, carrying food. Tammy's mother had a big bag of Fritos. The church itself was a square cinder-block building painted white. It looked like a convenience store. Its windows were made of the kind of frosted glass you find in restrooms. The only way you could tell it was a church was from the hand-lettered sign on the door, MARANATHA APOSTOLIC CHURCH ALL COME IN. I asked Tammy what "Maranatha" meant and she said she didn't know. Tammy would rather be at *my* house on Sundays, so she could look through Mama's jewelry, eat lemon meringue pie at my grandmother's, and stare at Baptists. She had made this plain. I'd rather be at her house, in general; she'd rather be at mine. We walked into her church.

"This way." Tammy was pulling my arm. Men sat on the right-hand side of the church. Women sat on the left. There was no music, no Miss Eugenia Little at the organ. Men and women sat still, staring straight ahead, the children sprinkled among them like tiny grave adults. The pews were handmade, hard, like benches, with high, straight backs. There was no altar, only the huge wooden cross at the front of the church, dwarfing everything, and a curtain, like a shower curtain, pulled closed behind it. A huge Bible stood open on a lectern with a big jug (of what? water?) beside it. More people came in. My heart was beating a mile a minute. The light that came in through the frosted-glass windows produced a soft, diffuse glow

throughout the church. Tammy popped her gum. Tammy's mother's eyes were already closed. Her pale eyelashes fluttered. Her mouth was moving and she swayed slightly, back and forth from the waist up. Nothing else was happening.

Then four women, all of them big and tough-looking, went forward and simply started singing "Rock of Ages," without any warning or any introduction at all. I almost jumped right out of my seat. Some of the congregation joined in, some did not. It seemed to be optional. Tammy's mother did not sing. She did not open her eyes either. The women's voices were high, mournful, seeming to linger in the air long after they were done. "Praise God!" "Yes, Jesus!" At the conclusion of the song, people throughout the church started shouting. I craned my neck around to see who was doing this, but the back of the pew was too high, blocking a lot of my view. They sang again. I had never heard any music like this music, music without any words at all, or maybe it was music without any music, it seemed to pierce my brain. I was sweating under my arms again.

The preacher, Mr. Looney, entered unobtrusively from the side during the singing. Initially, Mr. Looney was a disappointment. He was small and nondescript. He looked like George Gobel. Tammy had told me he was a security guard at the paper mill during the week. He spoke in a monotone with a hick accent. As he led us all in prayer—a prayer that seemed to go on forever, including everybody in the church by name—my mind wandered back to a time when I was little and our whole family had gone to Gulf Shores for a vacation, and Ashley and Paul were there too, and all of us worked and worked, covering Daddy up with sand, and Mama wore a sailor hat. By the end of the prayer, I was crying, and Mr. Looney had changed his delivery, his voice getting stronger and more rhythmical as he went into his message for the day. This message was pretty simple, one I had heard before. God's wrath is awful. Hell is real and lasts forever. It is not enough to have good intentions. The road to Hell is paved with those. It is not enough to do good works, such as taking care of the sick and giving to the poor. God will see right through you. The only way you can get to Heaven is by turning over your whole will and your whole mind to Jesus Christ, being baptized in the name of the Father, Son, and Holy Ghost, and born again in Glory.

"Does sprinkling count?" I whispered to Tammy. I had been sprinkled in the Methodist church.

"No," she whispered back.

Mr. Looney went on and on, falling into chant now, catching up his sentences with an "Ah!" at the end of each line. People were yelling out. And then came, finally, the invitational, "Just as I am, without one plea, but that Thy blood was shed for me, O Lamb of God, I come, I come!"

The stolid-looking young woman sitting two seats over from us surprised me by starting to mumble suddenly, then she screamed out, then she rushed forward, right into Mr. Looney's arms.

I twisted my head around to see what would happen next. Mr. Looney blessed her and said that she would "pass through to Jesus" by and by.

"What does he mean, 'pass through to Jesus'?" I was still whispering, but I might as well have been speaking aloud; there was so much commotion now that nobody else could have heard me.

Tammy jerked her head toward the front of the church. "Through them curtains, I reckon," she said.

"What's back there?" I asked, and Tammy said it was a swimming pool that people got baptized in.

And sure enough, it was not long before Mr. Looney pulled back the curtains to reveal a kind of big sliding glass door cut in the wall, with a large wading pool right beyond it, the kind I had seen in the Sears catalogue. Mr. Looney pulled the heavy young woman through the curtains and hauled her over the edge of the pool. The water reached up to about mid-thigh on both of them. I couldn't believe they would just walk into the water like that, wearing all their clothes, wearing their *shoes!* Mr. Looney pulled back the woman's long hair and grasped it firmly. Her face was as blank and solid as a potato. "In the name of the Father and the Son and the Holy Ghost!" Mr. Looney yelled, and dunked her all the way under, backwards. Although she held her nose, she came up sputtering.

Now people were jumping up all over the church,

singing out and yelling, including Tammy's mother, who opened her mouth and screamed out in a language like none I had ever heard, yet a language which I felt I knew intimately, somehow, better than I knew English. It was *my language*, I was sure of it, and I think I might have passed out right then from the shock of sheer recognition except that Tammy grabbed my arm and yanked like crazy.

"Get ready!" she said.

"What?"

"She's fixing to fall," Tammy said just as her mother pitched backwards in a dead faint. We caught her and laid her out on the pew. She came to later, when church was over, and then we all had dinner on the ground out back of the church. Later I sneaked back into the fellowship hall on the pretext of going to the bathroom, so I could examine the pool in greater detail. It was in a little anteroom off the fellowship hall, right up against the double doors that led from the sanctuary, now closed. It was a plain old wading pool, just as I'd thought, covered now by a blue tarpaulin. I pulled back the tarp. The water was pretty cold. A red plastic barrette floated jauntily in the middle of the pool. I looked at it for a long time. I knew I would have to get in that water sooner or later. I would have to get saved.

I was so moved by the whole experience that I might have actually broken through my invisible shield to tell Daddy about it, or even Ashley, but Mama met me at the door that afternoon with an ashen face and, for once, no makeup.

"Where in the world have you all *been?*" she shrilled. "I've been trying to call you all afternoon."

"We ate lunch out at the church," I said. "They do that." Out of the corner of my eye, I watched Tammy and her mother pull away in the battered blue car and wished I were with them, anywhere but here. I didn't want to know whatever Mama had to say next. In that split second, several possibilities raced through my mind:

1. *Grandmother really has died.*
2. *Ashley is pregnant.*
3. *Ashley has eloped.*
4. *Daddy has killed himself.*

But I was completely surprised by what came next.

"Your brother has been in the most terrible wreck," Mama said, "up in Virginia. He's in a coma, and they don't know if he'll make it or not."

Paul had been drunk, of course. Drunk, or he might not have lived at all, somebody said later, but I don't know whether that was true or not. I think it is something people say after wrecks, whenever there's been drinking. He had been driving back to W&L from Randolph-Macon, where he was dating a girl. This girl wrote Mama a long, emotional letter on pink stationery with a burgundy monogram. Paul was taken by ambulance from the small hospital in Lexington, Virginia, to the University of Virginia hospital in Charlottesville, one of the best hospitals in the world. This is what everybody told me. Mama went up there immediately. Her younger sister, my Aunt Liddie, came to stay with us while she was gone.

Aunt Liddie had always been referred to in our family as "flighty." Aunt Liddie "went off on tangents," it was said. I wasn't sure what this meant. Still, I was glad to see her when she arrived, with five matching suitcases full of beautiful clothes and her Pekingese named Chow Mein. Back in Birmingham she was a Kelly girl, so it was easy for her to leave her job and come to us. The very first night she arrived, Liddie got me to come out on the back steps with her. She sat very close to me in the warm spring night and squeezed both my hands. "I look on this as a wonderful opportunity for you and me to get to know each other better," Aunt Liddie said. "I want you to tell me *everything*."

But I would tell her nothing, as things turned out. This was to be our closest moment. The very next week, Liddie started dating Mr. Hudson Bell, a young lawyer she met by chance in the bank. Immediately, Liddie and Hudson Bell were *in love*, and Ashley and I were free—within the bounds of reason—to come and go as we pleased. Aunt Liddie asked no questions. Missie cooked the meals.

This was just as well with me, for I had serious business to tend to.

I knew it was up to me to bring Paul out of that coma. I would pray without ceasing, and Tammy would help me. The first week, we prayed without ceasing only after school and on the weekend. Paul was no better, Mama reported from Charlottesville. The second week, I gave up sitting on soft chairs and eating chocolate. I paid so much attention to the unfortunate Lurice May that she began avoiding me. Paul had moved his foot, Mama said. I doubled my efforts, giving up also Cokes and sleeping in bed. (I had to sleep flat on the floor.) Also, I prayed without ceasing all during math class. I wouldn't even answer the teacher, Mrs. Lemon, when she called on me. She sent me to Guidance because of it. During this week, I began to suspect that perhaps Tammy was not praying as much as she was supposed to, not keeping up her end of the deal. Still, I was too busy to care. I gave up hot water; I had to take cold showers now.

The third weekend of Mama's absence and Paul's coma, I spent Saturday night with Tammy, and that Sunday morning, at Tammy's church, I got saved.

When Mr. Looney issued his plea, I felt that he was talking right to me. "With every head bowed and every eye closed," he said, "I want you to look into your hearts and minds this morning. Have you got problems, brother? Have you got problems, sister? Well, give them up! Give them over to the Lord Jesus Christ. If His shoulders are big enough to *bear the cross*, they are big enough to take on your little problems, beloved. Turn them over to Him. He will help you now in this life, here in this vale of tears. And He will give you Heaven Everlasting as a door prize. Think about it, beloved. Do you want to burn in Hell forever, at the Devil's barbecue? Or do you want to lie in banks of flowers, listening to that heavenly choir?"

I felt a burning, stabbing sensation in my chest and stomach—something like heartburn, something like the hand of God. The idea of turning it all over to Him was certainly appealing at this point. Another week of prayer, and I'd flunk math for sure. The choir sang, "Softly and tenderly, Jesus is calling, calling for you and for me." Beside me, Tammy's mama was starting to mumble and moan.

Mr. Looney said, "Perhaps there is one among you who feels that his sin is too great to bear, but no sin is too black for the heavenly laundry of Jesus Christ, He will turn you as white as snow, as white as the driven snow, hallelujah!" Mr. Looney reached back and pulled the curtains open, so we could all see the pool. Tammy's mama leaped up and called out in her strangely familiar language. Mr. Looney went on, "Perhaps there is a child among you who hears our message this morning, who is ready now for Salvation. Why, a little child can go to Hell, the same as you and me! A little child can burn to a crisp. But it is also true that a little child can come to God—right now, right this minute, this very morning. God don't check your ID, children. God will check your souls." "Come home, come home," they sang.

Before I even knew it, I was up there, and we had passed through those curtains, and I was standing in the water with my full blue skirt floating out around me like a lily pad. Then he was saying the words, shouting them out, and whispering to me, "Hold your nose," which I did, and he pushed me under backwards, holding me tightly with his other hand so that I felt supported, secure, even at the very moment of immersion. It was like being dipped by the big boys at ballroom dancing, only not as scary. I came up wet and saved, and stood at the side of the pool while Mr. Looney baptized Eric Blankenship, a big gawky nineteen-year-old who came running and sobbing up the aisle just as Mr. Looney got finished with me. Eric Blankenship was confessing to all his sins, nonstop, throughout his baptism. His sins were a whole lot more interesting than mine, involving things he'd done with his girlfriend, and I strained to hear them as I stood there, but I could not, because of all the noise in the church.

And then it was over and everyone crowded forward to hug us, including Tammy. But even in that moment of hugging Tammy, who of course had been baptized for years and years, I saw something new in her eyes. Somehow, now, there was a difference between us, where before there had been none. But I was wet and freezing, busy accepting the congratulations of the faithful, so I didn't have time to think any more about it then. Tammy gave me her sweater and they drove me home, where Aunt Liddie looked at me in a very fishy way when I walked in the door.

"I just got baptized," I said, and she said, "Oh," and then she went out to lunch with Hudson Bell, who came up the front walk not a minute behind me, sparing me further explanations.

Aunt Liddie came back from that lunch engaged, with a huge square-cut diamond. Nobody mentioned my baptism.

But the very next night, right after supper, Mama called to say that Paul was fine. All of a sudden, he had turned to the night nurse and asked for a cheeseburger. There seemed to be no brain damage at all except that he had some trouble remembering things, which was to be expected. He would have to stay in the hospital for several more weeks, but he would recover completely. He would be just fine.

I burst into tears of joy. I knew I had done it all. And for the first time, I realized what an effort it had been. The first thing I did was go into the kitchen and fix myself a milk shake, with Hershey's syrup. And my bed felt so good that night, after the weeks on the floor. I intended to pray without ceasing that very night, a prayer of thanksgiving for Paul's delivery, but I fell asleep instantly.

When Mama came back, I hoped she would be so busy that my baptism would be overlooked completely, but this was not the case. Aunt Liddie told her, after all.

"Karen," was Mama's reaction, "I am *shocked*! We are

not the kind of family that goes out in the county and immerses ourselves in water. I can't imagine what you were thinking of," Mama said.

I looked out the window at Mama's blooming roses. It was two weeks before the end of school, before Ashley's graduation.

"Well, *what?*" Mama asked. She was peering at me closely, more closely than she had looked at me in years.

"Why did you do it?" Mama asked. She lit a cigarette.

I didn't say a thing.

"Karen," Mama said. "I asked you a question." She blew a smoke ring.

I looked at the roses. "I wanted to be saved," I said.

Mama's lips went into that little red bow. "I see," she said.

So later, that next weekend when she refused to let me spend the night out at Tammy's, I did the only thing I could: I lied and said I was going to spend the night with Sara Ruth Johnson, and then prayed without ceasing that I would not be found out. Since it was senior prom weekend and Mama was to be in charge of the decorations and also a chaperone, I felt fairly certain I'd get away with it. But when the time came for the invitational that Sunday morning in the Maranatha Church, I simply could not resist. I pushed back Tammy's restraining hand, rushed forward, and rededicated my life.

"I don't think you're supposed to rededicate your life

right after you just dedicated it," Tammy whispered to me later, but I didn't care. I was wet and holy. If I had committed some breach of heavenly etiquette, surely Mr. Looney would tell me. But he did not. We didn't stay for dinner on the ground that day either. As soon as Tammy's mother came to, they drove me straight home, and neither of them said much.

Mama's Cadillac was parked in the drive.

So I went around to the back of the house and tiptoed in through the laundry room door, carrying my shoes. But Mama was waiting for me. She stood by the ironing board, smoking a cigarette. She looked at me, narrowing her eyes.

"Don't drip on the kitchen floor, Missie just mopped it yesterday," she said.

I climbed up the back stairs to my room.

The next weekend, I had to go to Ashley's graduation and to the baccalaureate sermon on Sunday morning in the Confederate Chapel at Lorton Hall. I sat between my grandparents. My Aunt Liddie was there too, with her fiancé. My daddy did not come. I wore a dressy white dress with a little bolero jacket and patent-leather shoes with Cuban heels—my first high heels. I felt precarious and old, grown-up and somehow sinful, and longed for the high hard pews of the Maranatha Church and the piercing, keening voices of the women singers.

But I never attended the Maranatha Church again. As soon as my school was over, I was sent away to Camp

Alleghany in West Virginia for two months—the maximum stay. I didn't want to go, even though this meant that I would finally have a chance to learn horseback riding, but I had no choice in the matter. Mama made this clear. It was to separate me from Tammy, whom Mama had labeled a Terrible Influence.

"And by the way," Mama said brightly, "Margaret Applewhite will be going to Camp Alleghany too!" Oh, I could see right through Mama. But I couldn't do anything about it. Camp started June 6, so I didn't have time to pray for a change in my fate. She sprang it on me. Instead, I cried without ceasing all that long day before they put me and my trunk, along with Margaret Applewhite and her trunk, on the train. I tried and tried to call Tammy to tell her good-bye, but a recorded message said that her line had been disconnected. (This had happened several times before, whenever her mama couldn't pay the bill.) My father would be going away too, to Shepherd Pratt Hospital in Baltimore, Maryland, and Ashley was going to Europe.

Sitting glumly by Mama at the train station, I tried to pray but could not. Instead, I remembered a game we used to play when I was real little, Statues. In Statues, one person grabs you by the hand and swings you around and around and then lets you go, and whatever position you land in, you have to freeze like that until everybody else is thrown. The person who lands in the best position wins. But what I remembered was that scary moment of being flung wildly out into the world screaming, to land however I hit, and I felt like this was happening to us all.

To my surprise, I loved camp. Camp Alleghany was an old camp, with rough-hewn wooden buildings that seemed to grow right out of the deep woods surrounding them. Girls had been carving their initials in the railings outside the dining hall for years and years. It was a tradition. I loved to run my fingers over these initials, imagining these girls—M.H., 1948; J.B., 1953; M.N., 1935. Some of the initials were very old. These girls were grown up by now. Some of them were probably dead. This gave me an enormous thrill, as did all the other traditions at Camp Alleghany. I loved the weekend campfire, as big as a tepee, ceremoniously lit by the Camp Spirit, whoever she happened to be that week. The Camp Spirit got to light the campfire with an enormous match, invoking the spirits with an ancient verse that only she was permitted to repeat. At the end of each weekly campfire, a new Camp Spirit was named, with lots of screaming, crying, and hugging. I was dying to be the Camp Spirit. In fact, after the very first campfire, I set this as my goal, cooperating like crazy with all the counselors so I would be picked. But it wasn't hard for me to cooperate.

I loved wearing a uniform, being a part of the group—I still have the photograph from that first session of camp, all of us wearing our navy shorts, white socks, and white camp shirts, our hair squeaky-clean, grinning into the sun. I loved all my activities—arts and crafts, where we made huge ashtrays for our parents out of little colored tiles; swimming, where I already excelled and soon became the acknowledged champion of the breaststroke in all competitions; and drama, where we were readying a presentation of *Spoon River*. My canoeing group took a long sunrise trip upstream to an island where we cooked our breakfast out over a fire: grits, sausage, eggs. Everything had a smoky, exotic taste, and the smoke from our breakfast campfire rose to mingle with the patchy mist still clinging to the trees, still rising from the river. I remember lying on my back and gazing up at how the sunshine looked, like light through a stained-glass window, emerald green and iridescent in the leafy tops of the tallest trees. The river was as smooth and shiny as a mirror. In fact it reminded me of a mirror, of Ashley's mirror-topped dressing table back home.

And the long trail rides—when we finally got to take them—were even better than the canoe trips. But first we had to go around and around the riding ring, learning to post, learning to canter. The truth was, I didn't like the horses nearly as much as I'd expected to. For one thing, they were a lot *bigger* than I had been led to believe by the illustrations in my horse books. They were as big as cars. For another thing they were not lovable either. They were smelly, and some of them were downright mean. One big old black horse named Martini was pointed out to us early on as a biter. Others kicked. On a trail ride, you didn't want to get behind one of these. Still, the trail rides were great. We lurched along through the forest, following the leader. I felt like I was in a western movie, striking out into the territory. On the longest trail ride, we took an overnight trip up to Pancake Mountain, where we ate s'mores (Hershey bars and melted marshmallows smashed into a sandwich between two graham crackers), told ghost stories, and went to sleep finally with the wheezing and stamping of the horses in our ears.

Actually, I liked the riding counselors better than I liked the horses. The regular counselors were sweet, pretty girls who went to school at places like Hollins and Sweet Briar, or else maternal, jolly older women who taught junior high school during the regular year, but the riding counselors were tough, tan, muscular young women who squinted into the sun and could post all day long if they had to. The riding counselors said "Shit" a lot, and smoked cigarettes in the barn. They did not speak of college.

My only male counselor was a frail, nervous young man named Jeffrey Long, reputed to be the nephew of the owner. He taught nature study, which I loved. I loved identifying the various trees (hickory, five leaves; ironwood, the satiny metallic trunk; maple, the little wings; blue-berried juniper; droopy willow). We made sassafras toothbrushes, and brushed our teeth in the river.

On Sundays, we had church in the big rustic assembly hall. It was an Episcopal service, which seemed pretty boring to me in comparison with the Maranatha Church. Yet I liked the Prayer Book, and I particularly liked one of the Episcopal hymns, which I had never heard before, "I Sing a Song of the Saints of God," with its martial, military tune. I imagined Joan of Arc striding briskly along in a satin uniform to just that tune. I also liked the hymn "Jerusalem," especially the weird lines that went, "Bring me my staff of burnished gold, bring me my arrows of desire." I loved the "arrows of desire" part.

We all wore white shirts and white shorts to church. After church we had a special Sunday lunch, with fried chicken and ice cream. "I scream, you scream, we all scream for ice cream!" we'd shout, banging on the tables before they brought it out. (In order to have any, you had to turn in an Ice Cream Letter—to your parents—as you came in the door.)

On Sunday nights, we all climbed the hill behind the dining hall for vespers. We sat on our ponchos looking down on the camp as the sun set, and sang "Day Is Done." We bowed our heads in silent prayer. Then, after about ten minutes of this, one of the junior counselors played "Taps" on the bugle. She played it every night at lights out too. I much admired the bugler's jaunty, boyish stance. I had already resolved to take up the bugle, first thing, when I got back home.

And speaking of home, I'd barely thought of it since arriving at Camp Alleghany. I was entirely too busy. I guess that was the idea. Still, every now and then in a quiet moment—during silent prayer at vespers, for instance; or rest hour right after lunch, when we usually played Go Fish or some other card game, but sometimes, *sometimes* I just lay on my cot and thought about things; or at night, after "Taps," when I'd lie looking up at the rafters before I fell asleep—in those quiet moments, I did think of home, and of my salvation. I didn't have as much time as I needed, there at camp, to pray without ceasing. Besides, I was often too tired to do it. Other times, I was having too much fun to do it. Sometimes I just forgot. To pray without ceasing requires either a solitary life or a life of invisibility such as I had led within my family for the past year.

What about my family, anyway? Did I miss them? Not a bit. I could scarcely recall what they looked like. Mama wrote that Paul was back home already and had a job at the snack bar at the country club. Ashley was in France. Daddy was still in Baltimore, where he would probably stay for six more months. Mama was very busy helping Aunt Liddie plan her wedding, which I would be in. I would wear an aqua dress and dyed-to-match heels. I read Mama's letter curiously, several times. I felt like I had to translate it, like it was written in a foreign language. I folded this letter up and placed it in the top tray of my trunk, where I would find it years later. Right then, I didn't have time to think about my family. I was too busy doing everything I was supposed to, so that I might be picked as Camp Spirit. (Everybody agreed that the current Camp Spirit, Jeannie Darling from Florida, was a stuck-up bitch who didn't deserve it at all.) At the last campfire of First Session, I had high hopes that I might replace her. We started out by singing all the camp songs, first the funny ones such as "I came on the train and arrived in the rain, my trunk came a week later on." Each "old" counselor had a song composed in her honor, and we sang them all. It took forever. As we finally sang the Camp Spirit song, my heart started beating like crazy.

But it was not to be. No, it was Jeanette Peterson, a skinny boring redhead from Margaret Applewhite's cabin. I started crying but nobody knew why, because by then everybody else was crying too, and we all continued to cry as we sang all the sad camp songs about loyalty and friendships and candle flames. This last campfire was also Friendship Night. We had made little birchbark boats that afternoon, and traded them with our best friends. At the end of the campfire, the counselors passed out short white candles which we lit and carried down to the river in a solemn procession. Then we placed the candles in our little boats and set them in the water, singing our hearts out as the flotilla of candles entered the current and moved slowly down the dark river and out of sight around the bend. I clung to my New Best Friend and cried. This was Shelley Long from Leesburg, Virginia, with a freckled, heart-shaped face and a pixie haircut, who talked a mile a minute all the time. It was even possible that Shelley Long had read more books than I had, unlike my Old Best Friend Tammy back at home in Alabama, who had not read any books at all, and did not intend to. Plus, Shelley Long owned a pony and a pony cart. She had shown me a picture of herself at home in Leesburg, driving her pony cart. Her house, in the background, looked like Mount Vernon. I was heartbroken when she left, the morning after Friendship Night.

It rained that morning, a cold drizzle that continued without letup for the next two days. About three-quarters of the campers left after First Session, including everybody I liked. Margaret Applewhite stayed. My last vision of the departing campers was a rainy blur of waving hands as the big yellow buses pulled out, headed for the train station and the airport. All the girls were singing at the top of their lungs, and their voices seemed to linger in the air long after they were gone. Then came a day and a half of waiting around for the Second Session campers to arrive, a day and a half in which nobody talked to me much, and the counselors were busy doing things like counting the rifle shells. So I became invisible again, free to wander about in the rain, free to pray without ceasing.

Finally the new campers arrived, and I brightened somewhat at the chance to be an Old Girl, to show the others the ropes and teach them the words to the songs. My New Best Friend was Anne Roper, from Lexington, Kentucky. She wasn't as good as Shelley, but she was the best I could do, I felt, considering what I had to pick from. Anne Roper was okay.

But my new counselor was very weird. She read aloud to us each day at rest hour from a big book named *The*

Fountainhead, by Ayn Rand. Without asking our parents, she pierced all our ears. Even this ear-piercing did not bring my spirits up to the level of First Session, however. For one thing, it never stopped raining. It rained and rained and rained. First, we couldn't go swimming—the river was too high, too cold, too fast. We couldn't go canoeing either. The tennis courts looked like lakes. The horses, along with the riding counselors, stayed in their barn. About all we could do was arts and crafts and Skits, which got old fast. Lots of girls got homesick. They cried during "Taps."

I cried then and at other odd times too, such as when I walked up to breakfast through the constant mist that came up now from the river, or at church. I was widely thought to be homesick. To cheer me up, my weird counselor gave me a special pair of her own earrings, little silver hoops with turquoise chips in them, made by Navajos.

Then I got bronchitis. I developed a deep, thousand-year-old Little Match Girl cough that started way down in my knees. Because of this cough, I was allowed to call my mother, and to my surprise, I found myself asking to come home. But Mama said no. She said,

We always finish what we start, Karen.

So that was that. I was taken into town for a penicillin shot, and started getting better. The sun came out too.

But because I still had such a bad cough, I did not have to participate in the all-camp Game Day held during the third week of Second Session. I was free to lounge in my upper bunk and read the rest of *The Fountainhead,* which I did. By then I had read way ahead of my counselor. I could hear the screams and yells of the girls out on the playing fields, but vaguely, far away. Then I heard them all singing, from farther up the hill, and I knew they had gone into Assembly to give out the awards. I knew I was probably expected to show up at Assembly too, but somehow I just couldn't summon up the energy. I didn't care who got the awards. I didn't care which team won—the Green or the Gold, it was all the same to me—or which cabin won the ongoing competition among cabins. I didn't even care who was Camp Spirit. Instead I lolled on my upper bunk and looked at the turning dust in a ray of light that came in through a chink in the cabin. I coughed. I felt that I would die soon.

This is when it happened.

This is when it always happens, I imagine—when you least expect it, when you are least prepared.

Suddenly, as I started at the ray of sunshine, it intensified, growing brighter and brighter until the whole cabin was a blaze of light. I sat right up, as straight as I could. I crossed my legs. I knew I was waiting for something. I knew something was going to happen. I could barely breathe. My heart pounded so hard I feared it might jump right out of my chest and land on the cabin floor. I don't know how long I sat there like that, waiting.

"Karen," He said.

His voice filled the cabin.

I knew immediately who it was. No question. For one thing, there were no men at Camp Alleghany except for Mr. Grizzard, who cleaned out the barn, and Jeffrey Long, who had a high, reedy voice.

This voice was deep, resonant, full of power.

"Yes, Lord?" I said.

He did not speak again. But as I sat there on my upper bunk I was filled with His presence, and I knew what I must do.

I jumped down from my bunk, washed my face and brushed my teeth at the sink in the corner, tucked in my shirt, and ran up the hill to the assembly hall. I did not cough. I burst right in through the big double doors at the front and elbowed old Mrs. Beemer aside as she read out the results of the archery meet to the rows of girls in their folding chairs.

Mrs. Beemer took one look at me and shut her mouth.

I opened my mouth, closed my eyes, and started speaking in Tongues of Fire.

I came to in the infirmary, surrounded by the camp nurse, the doctor from town, the old lady who owned the camp, the Episcopal chaplain, my own counselor, and several other people I didn't even know. I smiled at them all. I felt great, but they made me stay in the infirmary for two more days to make sure I had gotten over it. During this time I was given red Jell-O and Cokes, and the nurse took my temperature every four hours. The chaplain talked to me for a long time. He was a tall, quiet man with wispy white hair that stood out around his head. I got to talk to my mother on the telephone again, and this time she promised me a kitten if I would stay until the end of camp. I had always, always wanted a kitten, but I had never been allowed to have one because it would get hair on the upholstery and also because Ashley was allergic to cats.

"What about Ashley?" I asked.

"Never you mind," Mama said.

So it was decided. I would stay until the end of camp, and Mama would buy me a kitten.

I got out of the infirmary the next day and went back to my cabin, where everybody treated me with a lot of deference and respect for the rest of Second Session, choosing me first for softball, letting me star in Skits. And at the next-to-last campfire, I was named Camp Spirit. I got to run forward, scream and cry, but it was not as good as it would have been if it had happened First Session. It was an anticlimax. Still, I did get to light the very last campfire, the Friendship Night campfire, with my special giant match and say ceremoniously:

Kneel always when you light a fire,
Kneel reverently,

And thankful be
For God's unfailing majesty.

Then everybody sang the Camp Spirit song. By now, I was getting *really tired of singing.* Then Anne Roper and I sailed each other's little birchbark boats off into the night, our candles guttering wildly as they rounded the bend.

All the way home on the train the next day, I pretended to be asleep while I prayed without ceasing that nobody back home would find out I had spoken in Tongues of Fire. For now it seemed to me an exalted and private and scary thing, and somehow I knew it was not over yet. I felt quite sure that I had been singled out for some terrible, holy mission. Perhaps I would even have to *die*, like Joan of Arc. As the train rolled south through Virginia on that beautiful August day, I felt myself moving inexorably toward my Destiny, toward some last act of my own Skit which was yet to be played out.

The minute I walked onto the concrete at the country club pool, I knew that Margaret Applewhite (who had flown home) had told everybody. Dennis Jones took one look at me, threw back his head, and began to gurgle wildly, clutching at his stomach. Tommy Martin ran out on the low board, screamed in gibberish, and then flung himself into the water. Even I had to laugh at him. But Paul and his friends teased me in a more sophisticated manner.

"Hey, Karen," one of them might say, clutching his arm, "I've got a real bad tennis elbow here, do you think you can heal it for me?"

I was famous all over town. I sort of enjoyed it. I began to feel popular and cute, like the girls on *American Bandstand*.

But the kitten was a disaster. Mama drove me out in the county one afternoon in her white Cadillac to pick it out of a litter that the laundry lady's cat had had. The kittens were all so tiny that it was hard to pick—little mewling, squirming things, still blind. Drying sheets billowed all about them, on rows of clotheslines. "I want *that* one," I said, picking the smallest, a teeny little orange ball. I named him Sandy. I got to keep Sandy in a shoe box in my room, then in a basket in my room. But as time passed (Ashley came home from Europe, Paul went back to W&L) it became clear to me that there was something terribly wrong with Sandy. Sandy *mewed too much*, not a sweet mewing, but a little howl like a lost soul. He never purred. He wouldn't grow right either, even though I fed him half-and-half. He stayed little and jerky. He didn't act like a cat. One time I asked my mother, "Are you *sure* Sandy is a regular cat?" and she frowned at me and said, "Well, of *course* he is, what's the matter with you, Karen?" but I was not so sure. Sandy startled too easily. Sometimes he would leap straight up in the air, land on all four feet, and just stand there quivering, for no good reason at all. While I was watching him do this one day, it came to me.

Sandy was a Holy Cat. He was possessed by the spirit, as I had been. I put his basket in the laundry room. I was fitted for my aqua semiformal dress, and wore it in Aunt Liddie's wedding. Everybody said I looked grown-up and beautiful. I got to wear a corsage. I got to drink champagne. We had a preschool meeting of the Sub-Deb Club, and I was elected secretary. I kept trying to call Tammy, from pay phones downtown and the phone out at the country club, so Mama wouldn't know, but her number was still out of order. Tammy never called me.

Then Ashley invited me to go to the drive-in movie with her and her friends, just before she left for Sweet Briar. The movie was *All That Heaven Allows*, which I found incredibly moving, but Ashley and her friends smoked cigarettes and giggled through the whole thing. They couldn't be serious for five minutes. But they were being real nice to me, so I volunteered to go to the snack bar for them the second or third time they wanted more popcorn. On the way back from the snack bar, in the window of a red Thunderbird with yellow flames painted on its hood, I saw Tammy's face.

I didn't hesitate for a minute. I was *so* glad to see her! "Tammy!" I screamed. The position of My Best Friend was, of course, vacant. I ran right over to the Thunderbird, shifted all the popcorn boxes over to my left hand, and flung open the door. And sure enough, there was Tammy, *with the whole top of her sundress down.* It all happened in an instant. I saw a boy's dark hair, but not his face—his head was in her lap.

Tammy's breasts loomed up out of the darkness at me. They were perfectly round and white, like tennis balls. But it seemed to me that they were too high up to look good. They were too close to her chin.

Clearly, Tammy was Petting. And in a flash I remembered what Mama had told me about Petting, that

a nice girl does not Pet. It is cruel to the boy to allow him to Pet, because he has no control over himself. He is just a boy. It is all up to the girl. If she allows the boy to Pet her, then he will become excited, and if he cannot find relief, then the poison will all back up into his organs, causing pain and sometimes death.

I slammed the car door. I fled back to Ashley and her friends, spilling popcorn everyplace as I went.

On the screen, Rock Hudson had been Petting too. Now we got a close-up of his rugged cleft chin. "Give me one of those cigarettes," I said to Ashley, and without batting an eye, she did. After three tries, I got it lit. It tasted great.

The next day, Ashley left for Sweet Briar, and soon after that, my school started too. Whenever I passed Tammy in the hall, we said hello, but did not linger in conversation. I was put in the Gifted and Talented group for English and French. I decided to go out for JV cheerleader. I practiced and practiced and practiced. Then, one day in early September, my cat Sandy—after screaming out and leaping straight up in the air—ran out into the street in front of our house and was immediately hit by a Merita bread truck.

I knew it was suicide.

I buried him in the backyard, in a box from Rich's department store, along with Ashley's scarab bracelet which I had stolen sometime earlier. She wondered for years whatever happened to that bracelet. It was her favorite.

I remember how relieved I felt when I had smoothed the final shovelful of dirt over Sandy's grave. Somehow, I knew, the last of my holiness, of my chosenness, went with him. Now I wouldn't have to die. Now my daddy would get well, and I would make cheerleader, and go to college. Now I could grow up, get breasts, and have babies. Since then, all these things have happened. But there are moments yet, moments when in the midst of life a silence falls, and in these moments I catch myself still listening for that voice. *"Karen,"* He will say, and I'll say, "Yes, Lord. Yes."

Dreamers

I got a wife, which might surprise you, seeing as how I'm still so young and all. I got a baby too. Well I've got this wife. She looks like Ann-Margret too. But her name is Kim. We live with my moma and my sister, Janice. You ought to see this picture of my wife we've got up on top of the TV, Kim making her debut which is something she honest to God did three years ago in Rocky Mount. In the picture, Kim is wearing a long white floor-length fancy dress and pearls and little pearl earrings. She's got lace and flowers and all in her hair. She looks great. She is staring right out of that picture frame and when you look at the picture, it's like her eyes will follow you all over the room. You can sit on the couch or you can sit in the recliner. There is a famous painting like that too. I remember this from Art in high school. Anyway when I look at Kim's deb picture in its fancy frame, I like to think that she is looking into the future. That she is looking for me.

She found me about one year later. See, first Kim was a deb and then she went to St. Marys College over here in Raleigh, they have got a lot of debs at St. Marys. Kim's mother and two of her aunts went to St. Marys too, what chance did she have. They make a daisy chain when you graduate from St. Marys, and hand it over to the juniors. I have seen a picture of this, Kim's mother holding up the daisy chain. She is younger in the picture, but she does not look like Ann-Margret. Her collarbones stick out. She looks like a bitch which she is, no wonder Kim's daddy split.

Kim herself did not get to do the chain thing. She got pregnant, and married me.

See, last spring I went over there to St. Marys with Creative Landscaping. I was working two jobs then because Daddy was in the hospital at Dorothea Dix which he has been in and out of for years. He sees things. He hears them too. You can't keep him on his medicine. It is another story. Anyway I had already graduated from Broughton High and I was working these two jobs, so I went over there to St. Marys College with Creative Landscaping. We had a contract with them. They have these big long rows of bushes going everyplace, and if any one of those bushes started dying, we would come in and take it out and replace it with another one the same size. And we used to change the flowers around the fountain and the sundial and all along there in front of the chapel, whatever was prettiest that was in season, first daffodils then pansies then petunias then gardenias then mums in the fall. Something is always blooming at St. Marys College. Everything is the same size. It looks great. So I liked that job a lot, I like to see things looking good. In fact I got to thinking I might go over to State and get a degree in that. I had thought English, before I got the Creative Landscaping job. I had $1,900 saved up, but then I got married.

I used to have this weird little man teacher at Broughton High named Mr. Burton, he thought I was great in English. When we did Shakespeare, we had to write a sonnet. The end of my sonnet was,

So let me be a candle burning bright
With hope and love against the coming night.

That is a couplet. It knocked him out. He gave me an A plus. Then he came over and sat down next to me in the cafeteria at Lunch. He had this big salad. He said he was a vegetarian.

"Joe," he said next, "what are your plans for next year?"

"Work, I reckon," I said.

He said he hoped I was considering college. He hoped I had looked into the possibilities for financial aid. But on account of what had happened with Daddy and all, I had dropped out once already. So my grades were not too hot. For a while there I couldn't concentrate. I got plenty of Cs.

But then Moma quit drinking and got another job and I came back for senior year.

But I did not want to get into all this with Mr. Burton.

He had a pink shirt on. This buddy of mine, Roger, always said Mr. Burton was gay but I don't think so. "I'll be glad to write you a recommendation anytime, anyplace," Mr. Burton said. He had salad in his teeth. "Do you *want* to go to college?" he asked me. We stood up with our trays.

"It is my dream," I said.

As soon as I said this, I knew it was true. And who knows? I might get there yet. But I've got a family to take care of now. I try to do the right thing.

So this is how I met Kim. It was spring, everything blooming and the right size on the campus at St. Marys College. Azaleas, forsythia, periwinkle, you name it, it was blooming. We were edging the walks. So that day I had to work bent over which made my jeans too tight. I took my wallet and my knife out of my pocket and put them up in the crotch of a tree. Then when I got halfway home I remembered this, so I had to get off the Beltline and turn all the way around and go back. So I was pissed. It was hot, and I was pissed. I went back over there.

Now the grass was full of girls, soaking up the rays. Classes must have been over for the day. Lord. Tits and ass and long, long legs, and all of them winter white. This was just about the first day it was hot enough to lay out, see.

Then I saw her. Oh lord. Kim was laying on her back

on her towel, wearing this little bitty pink bikini bathing suit. She had cotton pads over her eyes. She had this aluminum, I guess it was, reflector under her head, so she would get *more* sun. Oh lord. She was all pink and curvy. She looked as good as it gets. I got my knife and my wallet out of this crotch in the tree and put them in my pocket and then I just stood there. I couldn't of moved if you'd paid me. I stood there awhile and then two things happened real fast.

Kim sat up all of a sudden and the cotton pads fell down off her eyes. "What do you think you're looking at?" she said. But she did not act mad. She had a little line of sweat on her upper lip. She looked so good.

At the same time she sat up, this big security guard in a brown shirt and pants started across the grass toward us. "Hey, buddy!" he was hollering. They keep a real close watch on those girls. By then, though, I didn't care if he shot me.

"I'm looking at *you*," I said to Kim.

She crinkled up the corners of her eyes then the way she does and smiled at me, she was ready for adventure, I could tell.

"All right, buddy. The show's over." The security guard had me by the elbow, he was hustling me out of there. I looked back at Kim while he did this.

"Call me," she said.

Well, I did, of course. I was a regular Sherlock Holmes figuring out who she was and how to do it. I had to sleuth around. But she was my dream girl. I told her so, right off the bat.

"Don't even get in this truck unless you are going to take me seriously," I said the first time I picked her up. I had planned to say this. I had practiced saying it. My truck was the only truck parked along that half-moon driveway in front of the school, where you go to pick up your date. People were looking at it.

She climbed right in. "Where are we going?" she said.

I drove her up to Kerr Lake. We got some beer and some crackers and Vienna sausage and Velveeta cheese at a 7-Eleven on the way up there. We had a picnic. It was the best food I ever ate. On the way back, I played her my new Don Williams tape. It's real romantic. I was in love. By then it was dark out and we rode with the windows down. Kim scooted over and sat real close to me in the truck. She has this way of filling her skin so full of herself that she almost busts out, if you follow me. It's hard to explain. It is a very attractive feature though. Maybe you call it charisma. I went home and wrote a song about her.

We kept it up. I was over there at the college as much as I could be, whenever I wasn't working. Anytime I could get over there, Kim would go out with me. She could have had her pick and I knew it, boys from State, fraternity guys from Chapel Hill. But Kim wanted me. She wanted me even after her mother started taking a fit which she did soon enough. Her mother really got up on her high horse about it. She told Kim that she couldn't see me anymore, and said

I was a day laborer. I couldn't argue with her. I reckon I am one. I did not even try to tell Kim's mother about being in the Art Club or the Honor Council or what Mr. Burton said. Kim's suitemates thought it was all real romantic, they used to cover for her when she would stay out all night. Of course I couldn't take her over to my house because of my little sister, Janice, that I felt kind of responsible for. So we stayed at Days Inns, and like that. One time we went down to Morehead City and ate at Captain Tony's, right on the dock. Kim was not doing so hot in school by then as you can imagine. Exams were coming up. I reckon she would of flunked out if she hadn't of gotten pregnant, which she did.

"What do *you* want to do?" I asked her this when the EPT showed positive. What I wanted to do was marry her, but I didn't want to force her into anything.

She looked at me. Her brown eyes got big and sparkly. Again I felt that quality I was telling you about, like she might pop right out of her skin. "I want to have the baby," she said. Kim's dorm room was all full of stuffed animals and Care Bears and rainbow posters, and like that, so I was not surprised.

"Mama will just *die*," she said. Now I knew *that* was true too. Kim's mom always told her, Marry a surgeon. Kim hates her mom. Kim's dad left because he just couldn't take it anymore, according to Kim. Her older brother went with him, out to California. Kim's mom had already tried to get her father to write to Kim and tell her to stop dating me, but he would not. Instead he sent her a postcard from Hawaii that said, "Follow your bliss. Love, Dad."

So I was not surprised at the way Kim's mom acted. The only thing that did surprise me was my own family's reaction. My mother is a sweet woman, she was sweet even when she was drinking. Now she's got high sugar and can't. Anyway my mother just smiled and kissed me when I told her, but that night I heard her crying in bed like her heart would break, that real loud kind of crying which is embarrassing to hear. The only time I ever heard her do it before was when Gran-Gran died, and the first time Daddy went into Dix. Janice kicked me in the leg when I told her, this surprised the hell out of me. I mean, I practically raised Janice. I guess she is jealous of Kim or something. Still, they came around. And they have been sweet as can be ever since Kim tried to slit her wrists.

That was four months ago, when Stacy was two months old. I was working two jobs, one at Creative Landscaping and one at Copy Quick, and we had a room in a boardinghouse down on Hillsborough Street. But things were not going so good. For one thing, Kim's mom had cut her off, I mean entirely. She didn't call on the telephone, she didn't come over to see the baby.

"I might as well be *dead*," Kim said. She stuck out her full bottom lip and her pretty brown eyes filled with tears.

"You've got *me*," I said. Between us on the bed in the room on Hillsborough Street, Stacy cooed and cooed. She held on to my finger. Sirens were screaming out in the street.

Kim looked at me. "I can't live like this," she said all of a sudden. "I just can't." She started crying.

Later that week was when she tried to slit her wrists, with a Trac II razor thank God, so it didn't work too good. The social worker at the hospital said she might not of really meant it. He said we needed some additional support. He called Kim's mother but even then she wouldn't talk on the phone to her daughter, heart of steel. Then Janice moved in the bedroom with Moma and we moved in with them, so Moma and Janice can watch the baby and Kim can get out some. Now Kim has got a part-time job at Tanfastic. But she still cries a lot, and she won't say why. The doctor says it is hormones, Moma says it's the blues. Anyway this is common, after a baby. It's been on TV. You can't blame Kim either. Her life is different from what it was. At her mother's house in Rocky Mount, for instance, they have five bed-rooms and wall-to-wall carpet. I know this.

But Kim hasn't got it *too* bad since we moved over here. She put Stacy on a bottle so she's got her figure back, and she's real tan. She looks great. And she doesn't have to do a thing except play with Stacy and watch TV. It's a funny thing, before we got married, I did not have any idea that Kim watched so much TV. I used to read books all the time myself. I can read the hell out of a book. But Kim doesn't like for me to read too much, she says it makes her feel left out. I am mostly too tired now, anyway. Now what we do is, she watches TV and I watch her. Janice is dating somebody now, she's gone a lot. Moma is in her room. I lay on the couch watching Kim watch TV and little Stacy lays on my chest. Stacy loves this. She's a little doll. She has this funny snuffly breath and a sweet milk smell. Stacy is one of those real solid babies with a round head and big round eyes. Her cheeks stick out. Now she sits up by herself, it won't be long until she is all over the place, Moma says.

On Sundays when I'm off work, me and Kim will go for a long ride in the truck, we put Stacy in her carrier between us on the seat. We might drive over to Chapel Hill or Rocky Mount, eat some tacos. We might take all day and drive up on the Blue Ridge Parkway. I can't ever figure out how they got all those rocks up there, to build those walls along the Parkway. It is amazing. It looks good too. I love riding along like this, looking out at some scenery, looking over at Kim, looking down at Stacy just sleeping away. It makes Stacy sleep, to go riding.

It makes her sleep to lay on my chest too as I was saying, we do that most nights. Stacy will snuffle and hold on tight to my finger even when she's asleep. I look at Kim and her face is beautiful in the pale blue light of the TV. She watches TV real hard, like she's taking a class or something. Stacy snuffles. This is my family. I am the man of the house.

Only, this morning something happened that worries

me some, it's hard to say why. Me and Kim were on our way to work and we drove in the Biscuit Kitchen like always. Mornings are a drag because you've got so much to do then, Kim has got to spend plenty of time dressing because she's got to look real good for her job at Tanfastic. It's like, part of the job. So I get Stacy up and change her and give her a bottle. She's got these little yellow pajamas with rabbits on them. I fix Moma her Diet Pepsi and take it in there and put it on the nightstand for her when I wake her up, which is the last thing I do before we go out and get in the truck and head for the Biscuit Kitchen. It's early, foggy and misty all over Raleigh. The arc lights are still on in Cameron Village when we drive by there, they make a misty pink glow in the fog, like fairyland. We drive past NC State, we drive past St. Marys.

We get to Biscuit Kitchen and pull up to the speaker and Kim orders a Coke and a sausage biscuit. I order two biscuits with steak and onions and one ham biscuit and a big Sprite. I won't get a lunch break at Copy Quick until 1:30, don't ask me why, so I have to eat a lot. Also, I am still growing. Anyway, we've ordered these biscuits and we're just sitting there in the truck waiting for our turn to drive to the little window and get them. We are listening to this REM tape but all of a sudden Kim reaches out and ejects it. Kim is not what you call a morning person. I have got the hang of this now, I try not to say too much, just let her slide into the day.

"I had a dream about you last night," Kim says.

"Oh, yeah," I say. "Just what was I doing in this dream?" I ask. I reach over and feel of her.

Kim pushes my hand away but I can tell she likes it, she is smiling at me. "Something like that," she says. Kim is smiling very sexy at me, she looks great this morning.

I say "Hey!" all of a sudden because now I remember *my* dream, which I would not of remembered if Kim hadn't said that. Gran-Gran always said if you don't tell your dreams you will lose them, and I reckon I was about to do that, lose the dream I mean. But now I get upset, because it was an awful dream. I remember it all now. I'm looking at Kim. The dream comes clear as day. "I dreamed we were in a motel someplace, you and me," I tell her, "and this guy came in."

"What guy?" Kim asks. She looks very interested in my dream.

"That's the weird part," I tell her. "I don't know the guy. I mean, I can't place him. I think I've seen him around, though. He looked kind of familiar."

"What does he look like?" Kim asks.

"Well, he's kind of a big guy," I tell her, "with long hair and a moustache. . . ."

"What color hair?" she interrupts me.

"Black," I say. "Definitely black. He looks like he might be part Indian or something, you know?"

Kim nods. She is looking at me the way she looks at TV. "Then what happened?" she asks.

"Hey." I start laughing. "Hey! This is *my* dream," I remind her. But the next part of the dream is hard to tell. "Well, what happens next is, this guy comes in the motel room, like I told you. We aren't doing anything in particular. We're just sitting there in this motel room."

"What's he wearing? The guy, I mean."

"A suit," I say. It all comes back to me like it was happening now. "Anyway he's got on this suit and he's a little bit older than we are, and for some reason, like I said, I kind of know him, it's like maybe I did a landscaping job for him or something, and so I say, 'Let me introduce you to my wife.'"

This is the bad part.

"But he says, 'We've already met.' Then he comes over and throws you down on the bed and starts kissing you like crazy."

"What?" Now Kim is staring at me in that skin-busting way I was telling you about before. Slowly, a big grin comes over her face and her cheeks turn red underneath her tan, like she's actually been caught in bed with this guy, like she is embarrassed.

Behind us in the line of cars, all these people start blowing their horns. So I throw the truck in gear and cruise up to the window and we get our biscuits and our drinks. All of this costs $7.41. Sun is breaking through the fog by the time I pull back out on Wade Avenue. While I'm driving up Wade Avenue I look over at Kim, her hair is all clean and shiny in the sunlight. Actually, she has got a lot of blond hairs and red hairs mixed in with the brown. She's eating her biscuit in tiny little bites. And she is still blushing, which makes me mad.

"Listen, Kim," I say. "You didn't do anything. It wasn't even your dream. It was *my dream*, remember?" Kim can tell I am getting upset now, so she slides over and gives me a big sexy kiss on the neck and puts her hand on my leg. "You silly," she says. We ride up Wade Avenue like that. I pull over in front of Tanfastic, and Kim gives me another kiss before she gets out of the truck. But I don't know. I still think she thinks it's her dream, and I still feel weird about it.

The Interpretation
of Dreams

For Ann Moss

Melanie stands dreaming against the open door, the entrance to Linens N' Things in the outlet mall in Burlington, North Carolina. It's raining. Melanie loves how the rain sounds drumming down on the big skylight at the center of the mall right over The Potted Plant and Orange Julius, it sounds like a million horses running fast, like a stampede in a western movie. She loves movies, she loves Clint Eastwood, now what if *he* came in the outlet mall right now and walked over to her and said, Excuse me, ma'am, I need a king-size bedspread in a western decor? She'd say, Why yes, come this way, sir, I've got exactly what you need. Only the trouble is that he won't come in probably, or any other real man either, men don't come to outlets unless of course they happen to work there, especially not to Linens N' Things, which is where Melanie works.

She's between men. Stan left Tuesday for a new job at WRDU in Raleigh, which has a soft country format. Stan the Man, they called him on the radio, what a joke. Melanie and him didn't really get along that good anyway, it was mostly a mistake caused by too many piña coladas. Stan turned out to be real self-centered like most media personalities, at least in Melanie's experience and she has known several. Like sometimes you'll have a boyfriend for a while and then you'll go out with his buddies after that, which was true of her and the guys at WHIT. All of their voices were so loud, plus they were kind of neurotic which is often true of artistic types. Melanie would like to steer clear of artistic types now and find a person who is basically down-to-earth, which she is.

Or maybe a healthy sports-minded man like Bobby of Bobby's Sport which is just opening up now in the corner space vacated by Pottery World. Mr. Slemp didn't have any heart for business after his wife died, they all watched her waste away before their very eyes, Mrs. Slemp, but she kept coming into Pottery World every day until the very last, when she had to go in the hospital. Mrs. Slemp was only forty-six years old. It was tragic, what a nice long marriage the Slemps had, they'd been at the outlet mall ever since it opened.

This is what Melanie wants, a sweet regular man she can watch TV with, and not have to put on her makeup or kick up her heels. A solid sports-minded man to be a role model for her son Sean, Lord knows he could use one even though he is almost grown up now and probably it's too late anyway.

Melanie sighs, nibbling a piece of her long red hair. Her sister says she's too old (thirty-seven) to wear it long, that a woman should cut her hair by age thirty at least. But men like it long. Melanie knows this. Long hair is sexy, short hair is not. Mr. Rolette, her boss, keeps calling to her but she doesn't answer him back, she's going to act like she doesn't hear, it's still early, and speaking of husbands, she's had three.

Some people might not count the first one since it was annulled, so it was like it never happened at all, like an abortion. She's had some of those too. But he was so sweet, her first husband. After she lost him she tried to be philosophical and think, Well, I was lucky to have him at all, but this was wrong. The fact is, he almost ruined her for anybody else. She'd been married and annulled by twenty, it was all downhill after that, or so it seems on some days like today when it's raining and she's feeling blue. He was the one she really loved. He was so intelligent. In fact he was in Army Intelligence that summer she met him, she was waiting tables at Wrightsville Beach, she'd just graduated from high school and he was a year out of college but real young, since he was so intelligent.

His name was Andrew, called Drew, he had gone to school up North. He was an only child whose parents lived in Greenwich, Connecticut, where the clocks are. Melanie never met his mother and she met his father only once, when he came down to Fayetteville to get them annulled. Drew's father looked like the guy on *Masterpiece Theatre.* He gave her a thousand dollars and kissed her on the cheek and said, "No harm done." This was not exactly true. Because never again did Melanie come across a boy who was so intelligent or could make her laugh so hard. He was going to be a professor, probably he's one now at some university up North, only Melanie doesn't know this for sure because his parents' phone is no longer listed in Greenwich. Sometimes over the years when she's been drinking, she's tried to call. Her second husband was nothing but a flash in the pan but at least she got Sean out of that one. Sean is the best thing that has ever happened in Melanie's life so far. And her third husband, Gary Rasnake, was cute but he was trouble from the word go, he wouldn't work and all he wanted to do was play, he loved equipment and gadgets for their own sake such as Weed-Eaters and remote-control toy airplanes and guns and cars and VCRs. They had the first VCR in Burlington, when nobody else had ever heard of them. A man ahead of his time.

"I'm coming," Melanie yells to Mr. Rolette. It's true she ought to go back in there now, Mr. Rolette's been nervous lately and the mall is filling up, it's getting real busy, everybody comes to the mall when it rains. The worst thing Gary Rasnake did was charge all those things on Melanie's Visa card and then leave town. She stopped payment of course, but still. Later, she found out that he'd done this before at least twice, once in Fort Walton Beach, Florida, and once in Spartanburg, South Carolina. But it wasn't all bad she guessed, they had some fun too even if she can't remember what they did exactly, it seems like such a long time ago.

And now she's getting old, too old to have long hair. It's time for another husband. The boyfriends she's had since Gary have not seemed like husband material, or else they just took off. Melanie is basically domestic, which is why she enjoys working at Linens N' Things. "Coming," she calls.

But as Melanie turns to go back in the store she catches sight of Bobby of Bobby's Sport coming to work. He wears a navy-blue running suit and bounces along on his brand-new athletic shoes like an advertisement for himself, which in a way he is. Melanie stands half turned in the door to watch him go by, and then to her surprise he gives her a big flashy grin. "Morning," he says. Bobby's teeth are so even and white, he must have had braces as a child.

"I saw that," says her best friend, Grace, who has been married to the same man for a million years so she is fascinated by this kind of thing.

"What? Nothing happened," says Melanie, but Grace says, "Huh!"

"Girls, girls, let's settle down now." Mr. Rolette claps his hands. They are getting ready for a back-to-school sale. Deborah Green at the cash register looks up from her book and glares at him. Deborah is an intellectual, working her way through school. Mr. Rolette sets the two black girls, LaWanda and Renée, to unloading sheets and scatter rugs for the back-to-school bin by the cash register, while Grace tidies up the bath area and Melanie waits on customers. She's good at it. Over the years she has gotten so she can match up a woman with a sheet in five minutes flat, it's like a sixth sense or something. In fact she's so good at it that she doesn't have to think much, she can go on dreaming although it's hard to say exactly what she's dreaming about, nothing special, it's still raining outside, all the people who come in Linens N' Things are dripping wet. That's the only bad thing about working at the mall, you miss so much weather. All you know is basically if it's raining or not raining, from the skylight which is frosted glass. Bobby of Bobby's Sport has a deep cleft chin which Melanie likes in a man.

At lunchtime she and Grace go to The Magic Pan. They always eat lunch together even though Grace is so persnickety. For instance she will say, There is too much cheese in this blue-cheese dressing, or, This Coke is flat. You can't satisfy Grace, which is probably one reason she is Melanie's best friend, opposites attract, and Melanie's easily pleased. Also they have worked together every day for the past nine years.

"Do you think Bobby is cute?" Melanie asks.

"Well, yes, I do think he is sort of cute," Grace says, "but he looks like he might be real bouncy, I think you ought to look for somebody older and more stable," says Grace. You can trust her to find some fault. Grace is married to her own high school sweetheart, Gene, a tall skinny man with big black glasses who is always worrying about things, he'd be the last man in the world that Melanie would be interested in, whether he was stable or not.

Grace fixes Melanie with her watery blue-eyed stare. "I think if I was you I'd try to look at all my options," she says, "and not just fall into something else."

Melanie opens her mouth and then shuts it. Grace means the best in the world of course, she just does not have a lot of personal tact, so what. Still, Melanie feels real down as they walk back to Linens N' Things together. Just the other day her sister said, "Melanie, you need to get a grip on things." Melanie knows her mother and her sister talk about her on the phone. They pass Shoe Town, Revco, The Casual Male, The Christmas Shoppe. Melanie thinks she would die if she worked in there and had to listen to Christmas carols all day long. They pass Deborah Green, sitting on the bench by the little fountain, reading a book. She doesn't look up. This reminds Melanie again of Drew, who was always reading.

"You go ahead," she says to Grace. "I'll catch up with you in a minute, I want to buy something to read."

Grace looks funny. "Huh!" she says.

But Melanie ducks into News and Notions anyway, it's not much bigger than a closet stuck in between The Christmas Shoppe and Marine Discount.

The very first book she picks up is a paperback named
How to Interpret Your Dreams, by dream expert Margery
Cooper Boyd. She went straight to it, it must be fate. "I'll
take it," she says, and pays the old man behind the counter,
who always stares at her bosom, and she buys a *USA Today*
also, to find out what's going on in the world, but as soon
as she reads the first page of *How to Interpret Your Dreams*
she's hooked. It's like Margery Cooper Boyd wrote this
book especially for her.

"Got a problem?" the book says. "Sleep on it. If you
know how, you can literally dream up a solution during
the night. The dreaming mind's ability to find creative
and logical solutions for unresolved problems has delighted
and intrigued man for as long as he has been in this
world. Without the ability to dream, it's doubtful that man
would have survived as long as he has. It is safe to say that
he certainly would not have attained dominance." Melanie
sits down on the bench in front of Belk's. "History is filled
with examples of how dreams have helped men and nations
to solve problems. Perhaps the best known examples are
Biblical—Pharaoh's dream of the lean and fat cows or
Jacob's dream of the sheaves and stars. In more modern
times, there are Robert Louis Stevenson, Samuel Taylor
Coleridge, Edgar Allan Poe, Mark Twain, Albert Einstein,
Wolfgang Mozart, and others who have had dreams."
Melanie blinks, she doesn't know who all these people are,
she can't remember anything about the pharaoh either.
Then she reads a lot of these dreams and what they turned

out to mean, and it is very interesting. Some dreams have changed the course of history. She doesn't care if she's late or not, she doesn't care if Mr. Rolette gets mad or not. Once you are able to accept your dreams as private messages from your subconscious, you open yourself up to a whole new world of self-understanding. You can get what you want!

"Listen to your dreams," writes Margery Cooper Boyd. This certainly ought to come easy to Melanie, who lives in a dream world anyway, everybody has always said so. In fact Mr. Rolette says it later that day, "Melanie, pay attention, you live in a dream world," when she marks the towels down wrong. The interpretation of dreams is done through symbols, everything you dream means something else. Melanie can't wait to start learning what they mean. Her dreams are full of symbols, sometimes at night she dreams so much she wakes up all worn out.

"Isn't it something?" she asks Sean later when they're eating dinner, tacos, something quick, she was too excited to cook much. Sean says, "Isn't *what* something, Mama?" in his normal bored voice, and she says, "Everything in your dreams means something else."

Sean smiles at her, the long slow smile which is the only characteristic he seems to have gotten from his daddy thank God, who was nevertheless attractive. "Mama," he says, "almost *everything* means something else."

Melanie just looks at him. "Well!" she says. Sean's hair is bleached and long on top, he has a rattail in back, his ears have been pierced so many times they look like Swiss cheese. Sean plays guitar, he looks like somebody who just knocked over a convenience store. But Sean is basically real smart and only a few people, mainly his teachers, know this. He'd drop dead before he'd let his friends catch him studying.

"What do you mean?" he asks, and so Melanie shows him the alphabetical listing, which is very complete, going from Abandonment, Accounts, Actor or Actress, Adultery, and Airplane all the way to Tomato, Tooth, Vault, Washing, Yellow, Youth, and Zoo. "Washing!" Sean says. "Who ever dreamed of washing?"

"Well, if they did, I'm sure it means guilt," sniffs Melanie, because it has occurred to her Sean might be making fun of her again.

"'Snow,'" Sean reads out loud. "'Snow is a symbol of purity. It can also symbolize sex. To dream of tracking through untouched snow expresses a desire for sexual intercourse.'"

"Give me that!" says Melanie, grabbing her book.

"So which is it, Mama?" asks Sean. "Sex or purity? How do you know?"

"You just have to trust your heart," Melanie says, "and go with your instincts that's all, that's what Margery Cooper Boyd says."

"Well, then it must be true."

He's teasing her all right, he's always teasing her, still they do have a wonderful relationship, considering, but sometimes it seems like it's gotten all turned around, like Sean's the grown-up here and she's the child.

"Listen, Mama," he says suddenly. "You remember Mr. Joyner?"

"Who?"

"Mr. Joyner, you know, my history teacher from last year. You met him at the end of school when you came over to see the concert."

"No, I don't believe I do," says Melanie, who can't recall even hearing the name before, of course she was busy last spring, what with Stan and the guys from WHIT.

"Well, now he's gotten a divorce, and he came up to me in the hall and asked me what my mother was doing these days."

Melanie just stares at him. A high school history teacher is not really her idea of a good time. "How old is he?" she asks.

"About forty-five." Sean lights a cigarette, he's been smoking since he was twelve, she can't do a thing with him really. "He's real nice, Mama, sort of an ex-hippie."

"Too old," Melanie says flatly, because no matter what anybody says, she's not over the hill yet. She can get somebody sports-minded and cute if she can harness her subconscious long enough to do it, but Sean stares at her through the smoke. "Maybe you could just talk to him sometime, Mama," he says, and she says, "Maybe so."

That night Melanie dreams that she is in a supermarket

where a lot of men are for sale and Margery Cooper Boyd is working the cash register. She says to Melanie in a Northern voice, "Take your pick, half-price today only, all sales are final." So in the morning Melanie dresses very carefully for work, the yellow dress with the black patent belt, the black patent shoes, she knows this dream is prophetic.

And sure enough, when he comes bouncing past Linens N' Things that morning, Bobby gives her a big wink. His intentions are perfectly clear.

"I saw that," says Grace, right behind her, and Melanie just can't resist, she tells Grace that actually she caused that wink herself, by harnessing her subconscious. Grace asks if this is some kind of new diet or what, and Melanie says, "No, silly, don't you remember my dream book? I've learned to interpret my dreams," but Grace turns up her nose and says Melanie ought to get a grip on herself, she ought to go to a doctor, it might be PMS. Grace's big blue eyes are watering the way they do when she thinks she's on to something. Melanie looks at her carefully. "Why, Grace!" she says suddenly, "I believe you're jealous!" As soon as she says it, she knows it's true. It's been true probably for years, only she never realized it before because she wasn't listening to her heart, she wasn't going with her instincts. Right now Grace is especially jealous because Melanie can interpret dreams, but not too jealous to hang around later while Renée tells Melanie what she dreamed last night. It was all in color, which proves Renée is very intelligent, according to Mrs. Boyd.

Renée says she dreamed she was supposed to go out to dinner with her boyfriend so she got all dressed up. She wore a red dress. In this dream she did her hair and then painted her nails and then her toenails, it seemed to take forever the way things sometimes do in dreams, and she was so hungry, she kept looking at the clock. Seven o'clock, eight o'clock, nine o'clock and still he didn't come, she was starving, she'd done her nails about seven times. Then finally at ten o'clock she realized that she'd been stood up and so she went to the refrigerator and got a frozen pepperoni pizza and put it in the oven to cook for dinner.

"Then what?" asked Melanie.

"What do you mean, 'what'?" says Renée. "That's *it*, honey. That's the end of the dream." It's not much of a dream, and Renée knows it. "I don't care if you like it or not," she says, all huffy. "It's *my* dream anyway."

"No, no, it's fine, Renée, I just need to concentrate on my interpretation, that's all." Melanie is getting nervous now because Grace and Deborah Green and Mrs. Small, the bookkeeper, have all gathered around to listen.

"Look up 'Dinner,'" says Grace, "or maybe 'Pizza,'" but there's no listing for either one.

"Oh, honestly!" Deborah Green acts like she knows it all. "The meaning is perfectly obvious. Renée is afraid her relationship's nearly over. She's afraid he's losing interest or something."

"*Roy?*" snorts Renée. "Roy is doing anything *but* losing interest."

"Maybe that's just what *you* think," Deborah says, which starts a big commotion that allows Melanie some time to consult Mrs. Boyd and think about Renée's dream. The interpretation, when it comes to her, is very serious. So she doesn't tell Renée until lunchtime, when she can catch her alone at Orange Julius.

"Renée, I'm afraid I have some bad news for you." Melanie is very formal. "I believe you're pregnant."

"No way I'm pregnant," Renée says, but her pretty eyes go wider, darker.

"You better find out," Melanie tells her, "because my book says that if a woman dreams of putting something in an oven, it means she is expressing a fear that she is pregnant or that she will become pregnant, or a desire to do so."

"Lord," Renée says. "I've got a tipped uterus, anyway."

"Well I'd find out if I was you," Melanie says. "It might be your subconscious trying to tell you something." Then Melanie's just standing there drinking her Orange Julius when Bobby comes by in a white terry-cloth jogging suit and introduces himself. He asks about business in the mall and whether she likes it here, and whether she runs.

"Runs?" Melanie says.

"You know, jog," says Bobby. "I just got in a new shipment of ladies' running clothes today."

"Oh yes, yes I do," says Melanie, who doesn't but plans to now.

"Well, I'd better get back to business," Bobby says. "Nice to meet you, see you around."

That night Melanie tells Sean that she is not a bit interested in meeting his ex–history teacher. She goes to bed early and dreams that she and Bobby are on a vacation in a tropical wonderland someplace like Hawaii, that they go swimming in the warm blue ocean and then they take a walk through a grove of orange trees and Bobby reaches up and picks some oranges which they eat and then they go dancing and so many men keep cutting in that Bobby gets jealous and makes her leave, but then her alarm goes off before she gets to the good part. It's a big rush to get Sean some breakfast and put on her makeup and concentrate on this dream, plus they are out of coffee. Melanie skims the book, Sean gets picked up by some of his friends in a hearse. Basically, water means sex and oranges mean breasts, so it's pretty clear what is going to happen next. Melanie wears her turquoise slacks and her turquoise and white sweater with the diamond pattern, just in case she sees him.

So she's late to work, but once she gets there it's very exciting because Renée runs in all happy and tells everybody that it's true, she *is* pregnant, she took the early pregnancy test last night, and that's not all either, her and Roy are engaged! Renée is glowing she's so happy, and Melanie is so happy for her.

But now it seems like everybody has a dream to tell her, suddenly she's famous in Linens N' Things. In fact Mr. Rolette speaks real sharp to her about it, which oddly enough reminds Melanie of another dream she had last night, it just pops back into her head all of a sudden, a dream that Mr. Rolette's house, the two-story colonial on Cedar Street where Mr. and Mrs. Rolette host the Christmas party every year, suddenly disappeared while she and Grace were walking up the driveway to it, carrying a covered dish. When Melanie tells Mr. Rolette this dream, he gets very mad at her and almost shouts, "Melanie, I think you ought to do this on your own time, it's very disruptive." Mr. Rolette has been nervous lately.

On Wednesday, everybody knows why. Mr. Rolette isn't there, but he has called Mrs. Small and said he will not be coming in for a while due to psychological factors. Mrs. Rolette has left him. When he got home last night, he found the note. And Mrs. Small, after she gathers them all together and tells them this, stares hard at Melanie. "Now how did you know?" she asks, and everybody else looks at Melanie too like there's something wrong with her, except Grace who has the morning off. Melanie spends the morning worrying whether she ought to go with her instincts so much or not, and whether Bobby is ever going to ask her out or if she ought to just go ahead and bite the bull by the horns and go up to Bobby's Sport right now and give him the opportunity.

Then Grace comes in and tells Melanie she needs to talk to her privately, so they go to the ladies' and lock the door. Grace has circles under her eyes. She has not looked too good lately. She's had this dream, she says, over and over again, and Melanie says, "Then it's probably significant." Grace smokes a Merit cigarette while she tells it. In the dream, Grace and Gene are in their living room and Gene is sitting at his desk paying the bills—"You know how worried he gets over money," Grace says, and Melanie nods—but after a little while his pen runs out of ink and he gets mad and throws it down on the floor. Then Grace brings him another pen and it happens again, several times. Then she wakes up.

Melanie flips through her book, past Owl, Park, and Peach. She pauses before she reads Pen out loud to Grace.

"Well, what does it say?" Grace is impatient, trying to see over Melanie's shoulder, but the light is bad in the ladies'.

"'Pens are phallic symbols representing the male organ,'" Melanie reads. "'If a man dreams of having a pen that has run out of ink, he may be expressing fears of impotency or that he is sterile.'"

"Well, I didn't know it was a *dirty* dream!" Grace says.

Melanie laughs. "Oh, Grace, it's not, it's all in your subconscious anyway, it says the same thing about guns and nails and pencils and cucumbers."

"*Cucumbers?*" Grace is furious. "I don't have to listen to this kind of dirty stuff," she says, leaving, pushing Melanie aside.

Melanie freshens her lipstick before coming out of the ladies', she can't see why Grace is so mad, Grace is her best friend, maybe Grace has got PMS. Melanie goes back over to the bath aisle where she's supposed to be pricing the merchandise, and finds a man there waiting for her.

"Mrs. Willis?" he says.

Melanie takes one look at him—at his longish thinning gray hair and his horn-rimmed glasses and his antique blue jeans and his tweed jacket with the patches on the elbow—and knows he's not there to pick out a shower curtain. She knows immediately who he is, Sean's ex–history teacher, Mr. Joyner. Mr. Joyner says he's been meaning to get in touch with her. He'd like to buy her a cup of coffee sometime soon and talk over Sean's future. He says Sean really ought to go to college and there is plenty of scholarship aid available if you apply in time and the right way. Melanie gives him a big smile. So this is all about Sean basically, it would be great if Sean went on to college which she hasn't thought too much about, she somehow thought he'd go straight into rock and roll. "I think it's real nice of you to be so interested," she says, and then Mr. Joyner makes a move. He steps closer and says, "I am interested. I'm very interested," in a significant way, and then he says, "Let's make it dinner."

"Well, I don't know." Melanie backs into the towels. Mr. Joyner's dark quick eyes make her uncomfortable. It's like he can see straight into her mind. He's grinning at her, he has a nice wide-open grin, she likes that in a man. "I'll call you," he says. Then he's gone, off down the mall, he's wearing Hush Puppies. Hush Puppies! Melanie would rather die than go out with a sixties person, they never have any money, and they're so old.

She's so upset she decides to walk right on up to Bobby's Sport and tell Bobby she's interested in his new line of women's running outfits so she does, she doesn't even tell anybody in Linens N' Things where she's going, who cares, Grace is mad at her and Mr. Rolette is at home having a nervous breakdown.

Bobby's Sport is neat and clean. It even *smells* new, like paint. What Melanie needs is a new start in life and a new running suit like this pink velour one. "How much?" she asks the girl, meanwhile looking and looking for Bobby, who doesn't seem to be anyplace around. "Eighty-nine ninety-five," the girl says, "but it'll last forever, I run in mine every day." This girl is wearing a white tennis outfit now so you can see her small firm breasts and her tight butt and the muscles in her arms and legs, men don't like too many muscles. She's very young, with a plain, friendly face. "You'll need to try it on," she says. "You might take a Large in that one."

Well! Melanie starts to say, who has never taken a Large in anything yet, but here comes Bobby suddenly, all smiles.

"I see you girls are getting acquainted," he says. "Linda, this is Melanie Willis, who works in Linens N' Things. Melanie, this is my fiancée, Linda Lewis."

"So pleased to meet you," Melanie says. Then she doesn't remember what she says next or how she gets out of that store, Bobby can just go to hell, suddenly she's out in the mall again and there's poor Mr. Slemp in front of Bobby's Sport looking so sad, looking the way she feels. She knows he's out there mourning Mrs. Slemp and thinking about all those years when Bobby's Sport was Pottery World.

"Why, Mr. Slemp, how are you?" Melanie makes a big effort, she feels so blue. Mr. Slemp looks terrible. He has egg stains on his white shirt.

"Well actually, Melanie, I'm pretty lonely," Mr. Slemp says, he sort of spits when he talks, in a very unattractive way, it's some kind of speech defect. "And I've been wondering if you'd care to come over and watch a movie on the VCR sometime."

Without one word Melanie turns and runs back to Linens N' Things, past Orange Julius and The Potted Plant and The Christmas Shoppe and News and Notions and The Casual Male, suddenly she can't even breathe anymore, too much is happening too fast.

Linens N' Things is very disorganized with Mr. Rolette gone, Melanie sees this right away. Deborah Green is reading a book, and Renée and LaWanda are giggling. Grace rushes up to Melanie and says, "Oh, Melanie, I'm so sorry I got mad at you, you're my best friend. Please forgive me. It wasn't even you I was mad at, I was just upset."

Melanie tries hard to forget about Bobby and Mr. Slemp and concentrate on Grace, who looks like she's still upset. "That's okay, honey," she says.

Grace pauses and looks all around and then steps closer.

"It's Gene," she says. "Gene is impotent, Melanie, he hasn't been able to do it for over a year."

"Well that's *awful*, Grace," Melanie says. "Has he been to a doctor?"

"He won't go," Grace says. "He won't talk about it either, not even to me. He walks right out of the room."

"Then I think *you* ought to go to a doctor," Melanie says, but Grace says he won't let her. She says Gene keeps the checkbook and there's no way she can go without him finding out. Grace's pale blue eyes look absolutely desperate.

"I'll loan you the money," Melanie says. "You can pay the doctor cash."

"Well, I don't know," Grace says. "I feel so *sorry* for him, Melanie. You know we went to the junior-senior together, we grew up practically next door, I don't know if I could go behind his back or not."

"Just think about it, honey." Melanie hugs her. "Let me help you any way I can." She can feel Grace's shoulder bones sticking out.

Then Grace straightens up and smooths out her skirt. "I feel a lot better since I told you about it," she says, but Melanie doesn't.

In fact she feels worse and worse as the afternoon goes by, and her customers say it's raining. So when things slack off she goes to stand by the door, feeling trembly and blue. When LaWanda comes out to ask her what it means if you dream you're flying, Melanie snaps at her, "I don't know," and LaWanda gives her a funny look and goes back inside.

Melanie wonders what she would even wear if she did decide to go out with Mr. Joyner, not that she would. Jeans? She'd have to buy some. The rain drums down on the skylight. *As soon as he walks past Orange Julius she sees him, wearing a blue Windbreaker and nice khaki pants and loafers, he looks sports-minded but not too sports-minded, he has that rugged all-American quality she loves in a man, a square jaw, a strong nose, his hands are not too small either. He notices her right away and comes toward her, his eyes never leave her eyes, he's smiling. "I'm relocating to this area from California," he says. "I've just bought one of those new townhouses out on Old Mill Road, it's furnished, but I need to buy everything else for it. Everything." "Come right this way, sir," says Melanie. "I've got exactly what you need."*

Desire on Domino Island

Preface

Some summers back, my friend Katherine Kearns, who was pregnant and bored at the time, decided that she wanted to write a romance novel. So she sent off to Silhouette Romances for guidelines, temporarily abandoned her pursuit of the Ph.D. in English at the University of North Carolina, and set to work.

Some of the guidelines follow:

Our Heroine is, preferably, an orphan. She is alone in the world. (Note: A brother is, in some cases, permissible, but only if he is retarded or has not found his way in life.) Our Heroine appears frail, but looks terrific when she gets dressed up. She is, of course, a virgin. She arrives alone in the lush, romantic Setting, where she encounters our Hero, who is preferably dark, brooding, and mysterious (although we have had some luck recently with stern Nordic sorts and hunky redheads). The initial encounter is tempestuous. Sparks fly, yet there is of course a mad underlying attraction. The Other Woman will be beautiful, desirable, and wealthy. She is, of course, a bitch. The Other Man will be nice, boring, well-meaning, intent upon saving our Heroine from the clutches of our Hero and the dangerous contingencies of the Plot. (Note: No other main characters will be permitted in this novel, *especially children.* Any necessary others, such as a faithful housekeeper, should remain as stereotypical as possible, so as not to detract from the romance.) The Plot will ensue, with the ten chapters growing increasingly shorter as tension mounts. At the climax, our Hero and Heroine realize that they are made for each other after all. The novel ends with their passionate embrace. (Note: At no time during this novel will they or anyone else every actually *do it*, nor will any specific body parts be mentioned.)

My friend Katherine did not sell her novel to Silhouette Romances, even though she came up with a wonderful heroine who inherited an old inn on Pawley's Island, South Carolina, and a mysterious saturnine artist who painted there. Her novel, *A Certain Slant of Light*, turned out to have two qualities that are not permissible: symbolism, and semicolons. But I, still intrigued by the guidelines, wrote this Silhouette Romance.

CHAPTER ONE

As the sleek motorboat slices through the aqua effervescence of Domino Bay to approach the pearly brightness of the beach, Jennifer surveys the lush scene before her with no small trepidation, and a hint of dismay creeps into her normally dulcet tone as she exclaims, "Captain! Oh, Captain! Why are you docking here in the middle of nowhere? Is there no settlement of any sort hereabouts? I had expected . . ."

But the captain won't say a thing! A native Georgian with an unfortunately cleft palate, he shoots a dark glance from beneath his surly brow at the clearly frightened young woman and mumbles something indistinguishable into his dark facial hair. He throws her bags on the beach. He heaves his bulk around.

Jennifer drums her small fingers rat-a-tat-tat on the hull of the shiny craft. Is it all a huge mistake, her coming here? But what else could she have done, considering the terrible fire that swept the home of her guardians (since their parents' mysterious deaths some twenty years ago, Jennifer and her retarded brother, Lewis, have been most carefully raised), killing both Aunt Lucia and Uncle Norm and destroying the entire perfect loveliness of their antebellum mansion, leaving Jennifer with only her small inheritance, her paltry background in microbiology, and the hunting lodge somewhere deep within the fastnesses of this fabled island.

"I had hoped . . ." But Jennifer's words are lost in the slap of the waves and the oddly shrill cries of the brilliant birds that wheel in the hot blue sky. Parrots and shy tropical creatures peek out at her from the shiny green leaves of the junglelike vegetation which threatens to engulf the beach; the shriek of an apparent panther is heard.

"Harg!" the captain barks. Clearly he wants to be quit of this spot before dark, wants to be back on the mainland hefting a brew with his rustic buddies.

Jennifer mounts the dock with a sigh, traverses its rotting length, and turns to wave a reluctant farewell to the enigmatic captain, who even now is rounding the great Grey Lady rocks which mark the harbor, slipping from her view. Well.

Although she is petite and somewhat fragile in appearance, a spark of mischief in Jennifer's eye belies the seeming frailty of her frame. Actually Jennifer is not frail at all! She's strong as an ox, and also she looks terrific when she gets dressed up. But right now she wears a lime-green T-shirt, a khaki wrap-around skirt, and espadrilles. Her wispy brown locks are caught fast in a gold barrette which used to belong to her mother. Jennifer hoists the weight of her luggage and trudges through the wet unwelcoming sand across the narrow beach and up a faint trail into the very jungle, vines slowing her progress as she bites her lip to hold back her brimming tears, as night begins to fall. . . .

CHAPTER TWO

Plucky Jennifer manages to set up her tent in a clearing beneath a giant live oak, where she eats a granola bar, lights her Coleman lantern, and soon is competently ensconced in the jungle wilderness.

But suddenly we note the rustle of plan fronds, the swish of savannah grass, the warning chorus of tree frogs. Footsteps are heard on the path. Jennifer, who was very nearly asleep, stands to face the invader. Jennifer's teeth clatter helplessly in the tropic night.

"Yes?" she cries bravely into the darkness. "Yes? Who's there?"

"Rock Cliff," comes the terse reply.

"I don't believe I have had the pleasure!" Jennifer casts open the tent fly.

Light streams out to reveal the rugged virile form clad in well-worn (tight) blue jeans, cowboy boots, and an old torn Brooks Brothers shirt open almost to the waist, unveiling the wealth of dark hair on the broad, muscled chest. Beneath the sable sweep of unruly hair and the decisive black line of his eyebrows, Rock Cliff's dark eyes flash fire above the prominent jut of his cheekbones. There is a touch of world-weariness in the little lines that web the marble wideness of his brow, a suggestion of tenderness and compassion which is offset by the fleshy cruel sensuality of his mouth, his strong white teeth. All his muscles bulge.

Now we are getting somewhere!

"Miss Jennifer Maidenfern?" he inquires rudely in deep masculine tones which send an unwonted tingle up Jennifer's spine.

"I beg your pardon!" she rejoins tartly.

"I received a communication from a Miss Jennifer Maidenfern not long ago, insisting that I vacate immediately the premises of Domino Lodge, where I have been in residence for the past ten months while finishing my novel," Rock Cliff continues. "I have now vacated those premises at enormous psychological cost, as I now find I am unable to complete my novel in any other surroundings. I urge you to reconsider."

It all comes back to Jennifer now. "I sent a letter to the occupant. . . ." she says slowly.

"I am the occupant," states Rock Cliff.

"I see." Jennifer realizes she is in danger of losing herself in the fiery depths of his eyes. "I'm terribly sorry," she says with an effort, "but that's quite impossible. I intend to stay."

"I am independently wealthy," asserts Rock Cliff. "I will pay any amount of money to purchase Domino Lodge." There's a sudden unaccustomed tremor in his voice now and we can tell how much this means to him, how his life of rich playboy decadence has left him empty and unfulfilled, how the completion of this novel will bring back his faith in himself.

Jennifer presses her trembling lips into a firm line.

"Good-bye, Mr. Cliff," she says. Attempting with shaking fingers to refasten the tent fly, she stumbles over a tortoise and falls backward suddenly, upsetting the lantern. The ever-alert Rock Cliff springs forward into the tent. Quickly he lunges past the terrified young woman to right the lantern and finds himself there suddenly on the tent floor beside her shy vulnerability and sweet trembling lips which he cannot help but cover with his own. The tent fly drops silently behind him.

So I can't see a damn thing! I want to be in that tent; I want to see it all. I want to know where he puts his hands. But here I am, reading, and there they are inside that tent, black opaque shadows moving against the flap, moving and thrashing and moving until at last he emerges with a muttered oath and stumbles off into the night.

CHAPTERS THREE, FOUR, AND FIVE

are a drag. Nothing much happening here except that Jennifer finally finds Domino Lodge (after several wrong turns, lots of boring flora on the trail) and meets faithful Irish housekeeper Mrs. O'Reilly, an amusing old alcoholic fond of misquoting familiar sayings, as in "Don't put all your eggs under a basset," page 62. Mrs. O'Reilly takes a liking to Jennifer right away, fixing her a hot buttered rum, some scones, some fig preserves. Jennifer eats with interest. Mrs. O'Reilly explains the blood feud which has always existed between the Maidenfern family and the deRigeurs on the other side of the island: an insult, a slight, a missing emerald. Mrs. O'Reilly praises the exemplary conduct of the recent occupant Mr. Cliff (Ha! Ha!), relates the complete history of Domino Island, and is working up to its geographic configurations when thank God she is interrupted by the surprise entrance of Charles Fine, the young Episcopal rector from the mainland, who has sailed over in his lovely sloop *The Dove* especially to bid Jennifer welcome.

"Welcome." He smiles.

"Why, thank you," Jennifer returns.

Jennifer cannot fail to notice this young bachelor's peaches-'n'-cream complexion, his lithe body, the warm sincerity of his soft blue gaze.

"If there is anything I can do to assist you," Charles Fine offers as he prepares to cast off, "anything at all . . ." His voice rings like a bell.

"I'll let you know," responds Jennifer. She watches him sail away until his boat is a mere black dot against the shimmering sea; she approves of him, Jennifer does, with all her fluttering heart, and she cannot understand the recent blush that climbed her features unawares when Mrs. O'Reilly mentioned that blackguard Rock Cliff. Oh! A hand flies up to Jennifer's mouth. It is, of course, her own.

CHAPTER SIX

So Jennifer settles in. The island sun paints a glint of gold on her plain brown locks and a dusting of freckles across the bridge of her nose. One morning she's hard at work refurbishing all the furniture in the east parlor when who should arrive but Rock Cliff! Jennifer—caught barefooted, no makeup, in one of her oldest frocks—tries to flee the parlor, but he blocks her way with his muscled girth.

"Not so fast, young lady!" drawls Rock Cliff. He actually appears to be amused; how dare he? "I've been thinking it over, and I feel I owe you an apology."

"I should say so!" snaps Jennifer. And then somehow she finds herself weakening, smiling up into those eyes. She can feel his breath on her skin. He leans down closer, closer, closer. . . .

Breaking free with a momentous exercise of pure will, Jennifer evades the virile visitor and commences to wash the woodwork on the other side of the room.

"Now Jennifer," he entreats, following her slim figure. "I want to make it up to you, Jennifer, if I may call you that. I'd like to take you out to dinner tonight."

Furiously, silently, Jennifer scrubs.

Rock Cliff edges even closer. "Come on now," he implores. "I feel a real connection between us, Jennifer. I sensed it from the first. I'm sorry I lost my head, but your nearness combined with the hot charm of the night . . ."

Rock Cliff has edged so close to Jennifer that she has been forced to retreat still further, has in fact climbed upon the windowsill itself, a precarious perch.

"Please, my dear," he begs passionately.

"I'm warning you, Rock Cliff!" shrills Jennifer, but then she tumbles—scrub brush, water pail, and all—straight onto the wide-planked cypress floor, overturning a handsome old desk, an ottoman, and Rock Cliff himself, who sprawls violently beside her in the sudden sea of suds.

Jennifer giggles infectiously. Rock Cliff catches her merriment and guffaws heartily, then turns to her with yearning eyes and clasps her wet torso firmly in his rippling arms. "My dear," he says.

"Oh, Rock," yields Jennifer, as . . .

CHAPTER SEVEN

"I might have known!" cries Monica deRigeur. "Look at you, Rock Cliff, down there on the floor all wet and unkempt in a compromising position!"

"Now wait just a minute," drawls Rock.

But Jennifer sees the emerald engagement ring on Monica's tapered digit.

"No!" Jennifer leaps up and stamps her petite foot. "Don't wait at all! Just leave! Both of you! I see right through you, Rock Cliff, you and your fashionable fiancée!"

Monica, by the way, is a real bitch wearing a low-necked

blue-flowered voile dress which does nothing to hide her voluptuous form. White high-heeled sandals and a strand of priceless pearls about her swanlike neck complete the ensemble. Her upswept coiffure is elegant, implicit, or imminent, or something. I give up. "Move it, lover boy," she directs haughtily.

"This is all a terrible misunderstanding," Rock states, but the force of Jennifer's grief ejaculates them both from the room.

CHAPTER EIGHT

Jennifer sends for her retarded brother and adopts a wild raccoon which she names Bruce, then nicknames Posy. (?)

CHAPTER NINE

Jennifer and Lewis are sunbathing on the secluded pink shell beach when here comes Charles Fine in his nautically white sloop, ready to propose to Jennifer. "I need a helpmeet," he explains earnestly, holding Jennifer tight in his strong ecclesiastical arms where she sheds a single tear upon realizing who it is she really loves.

"The cat is out of the bag now, I guess!" and, oh no, it's Rock Cliff who has been concealed behind some hydrangea bushes observing this tender scene. Rock Cliff's statement about the cat confuses Lewis, who becomes quite frightened and begins to weep openly. As Jennifer rushes to comfort her poor brother, helpful Charles Fine attempts to explain things to the irate Rock Cliff.

"You must not misconstrue . . ." Charles Fine begins.

"Misconstrue, hell!" shouts Rock Cliff, his fiery temper erupting totally since he has just broken his long-standing engagement to the beauteous Monica deRigeur only to find his dream girl in the arms of another man. Rock Cliff stalks off into the jungle just as lightning splits the summer sky and thunder rolls off the horizon, signaling the oncoming hurricane. A distraught Jennifer resists the fervent pleas of Charles Fine and Mrs. O'Reilly. She insists upon setting off immediately in search of Rock Cliff, and there she goes, accompanied only by her pet raccoon, into the dark wild jungle, into the eye of the storm.

CHAPTER TEN

just goes on and on! Jennifer is lost in the swamp, buffeted by the hurricane, set upon by wild dogs, defended by Posy, and drenched to the skin. Night falls. Jennifer finally takes shelter in a cave which strangely enough turns out to contain her parents' grave (!) as well as a sealed cask holding some long complicated To Whom It May Concern letter implicating the deRigeurs in her parents' death and explaining the curse of the emerald. *Who cares?* Jennifer tosses and turns in a restless doze yet feels strangely warm because of her parents' presence. At the first blush of dawn she sallies forth and retraces her steps through the jungle until she spots Domino Lodge at last through the dense fronds.

"Posy, we're home!" Jennifer tells the exhausted raccoon.

"And it's about time!" cries Rock Cliff, who has thought better of his hasty actions and has been scouring the jungle all night long for Jennifer. The bedraggled lovers rush toward each other and meet in a passionate embrace on the pink shell beach. Their clothes are all torn and wet, revealing their contours anew in the paleness of dawn. They kiss hungrily as Mrs. O'Reilly, Lewis, and Charles Fine steal out to the edge of the beach to share this happy moment. "Well, it's an ill wind which blows nobody," Mrs. O'Reilly observes with a chuckle, and Charles Fine reveals that he plans to teach Lewis to sail. Rock Cliff casts the unlucky emerald into the waiting waves; Monica deRigeur flies past in her private plane, bound for New York; Posy heaves a sigh of relief; and again the lovers embrace as, behind them, the sun rises out of the sea.

And that's it! I shade my eyes against the brightness of this sun, the glare off the water, but in vain: All I can see is the silhouette. Jennifer and Rock have nothing, nothing left—no faces, no bodies, not to mention fear or pain or children, joy or memory or loss—nothing but these flat black shapes against the tropic sky.

Intensive Care

Cherry Oxendine is dying now, and everybody knows it. Everybody in town except maybe her new husband, Harold Stikes, although Lord knows he ought to, it's as plain as the nose on your face. And it's not like he hasn't been *told* either, by both Dr. Thacker and Dr. Pinckney and also that hotshot young Jew doctor from Memphis, Dr. Shapiro, who comes over here once a week. "Harold just can't take it in," is what the head nurse in Intensive Care, Lois Hickey, said in the Beauty Nook last week. Lois ought to know. She's been right there during the past six weeks while Cherry Oxendine has been in Intensive Care, writing down Cherry's blood pressure every hour on the hour, changing bags on the IV, checking the stomach tube, moving the bed up and down to prevent bedsores, monitoring the respirator—and calling in Rodney Broadbent, the respiratory therapist, more and more frequently. "Her blood gases is not but twenty-eight," Lois said in the Beauty Nook. "If we was to unhook that respirator, she'd die in a day."

"I would go on and do it then, if I was Harold," said Mrs. Hooker, the Presbyterian minister's wife, who was getting a permanent. "It is the Christian thing."

"You wouldn't either," Lois said, "because she *still knows him*. That's the awful part. She still knows him. In fact she peps right up ever time he comes in, like they are going on a date or something. It's the saddest thing. And ever time we open the doors, here comes Harold, regular as clockwork. Eight o'clock, one o'clock, six o'clock, eight o'clock, why shoot, he'd stay in there all day and all night if we'd let him. Well, she opens her mouth and says *Hi, honey*, you can tell what she's saying even if she can't make a sound. And her eyes get real bright and her face looks pretty good too, that's because of the Lasix, only Harold don't know that. He just can't take it all in," Lois said.

"Oh, I feel so sorry for him," said Mrs. Hooker. Her face is as round and flat as a dime.

"Well, I don't." Dot Mains, owner of the Beauty Nook, started cutting Lois Hickey's hair. Lois wears it too short, in Dot's opinion. "I certainly don't feel sorry for Harold Stikes, after what he did." Dot snipped decisively at Lois Hickey's frosted hair. Mrs. Hooker made a sad little sound, half sigh, half words, as Janice stuck her under the dryer, while Miss Berry, the old-maid home demonstration agent waiting for her appointment, snapped the pages of *Cosmopolitan* magazine one by one, blindly, filled with somewhat gratuitous rage against the behavior of Harold Stikes. Miss Berry is Harold Stikes's ex-wife's cousin. So she does not pity him, not one bit. He got what's coming to him, that's all, in Miss Berry's opinion. Most people don't. It's a pleasure to see it, but Miss Berry would never say this out loud since Cherry Oxendine is of course dying. Cherry Oxendine! Like it was yesterday, Miss Berry remembers how Cherry Oxendine acted in high school, wearing her skirts too tight, popping her gum.

"The doctors can't do a thing," said Lois Hickey.

Silence settled like fog then on the Beauty Nook, on Miss Berry and her magazine, on Dot Mains cutting Lois Hickey's hair, on little Janice thinking about her boyfriend Bruce, and on Mrs. Hooker crying gently under the dryer. Suddenly, Dot remembered something her old granny used to say about such moments of sudden absolute quiet: "An angel is passing over."

After a while, Mrs. Hooker said, "It's all in the hands of God, then." She spread out her fingers one by one on the tray, for Janice to give her a manicure.

And as for Harold Stikes, he's not even considering God. Oh, he doesn't interfere when Mr. Hooker comes by the hospital once a day to check on him—Harold was a Presbyterian in his former life—or even when the Baptist preacher from Cherry's mama's church shows up and insists that everybody in the whole waiting room join hands and bow heads in prayer while he raises his big red face and curly gray head straight up to heaven and prays in a loud voice that God will heal these loved ones who walk through the Valley of Death, and comfort these others who watch, through their hour of need. This includes Mrs. Eunice Sprayberry, whose mother has had a stroke, John and Paula Ripman, whose infant son is dying of encephalitis, and different others who drift in and out of Intensive Care following surgery or wrecks. Harold is losing track. He closes his eyes and bows his head, figuring it can't hurt, like taking out insurance. But deep down inside, he knows that if God is worth His salt, He is not impressed by the prayer of Harold Stikes, who knowingly gave up all hope of peace on earth and heaven hereafter for the love of Cherry Oxendine.

Not to mention his family.

He gave them up too.

But this morning when he leaves the hospital after his eight o'clock visit to Cherry, Harold finds himself turning left out of the lot instead of right toward Food Lion, his store. Harold finds himself taking 15-501 just south of town and then driving through those ornate marble gates that mark the entrance to Camelot Hills, his old neighborhood. Some lucky instinct makes him pull into the little park and stop there, beside the pond. Here comes his ex-wife, John, driving the Honda Accord he paid for last year.

Joan looks straight ahead. She's still wearing her shiny blond hair in the pageboy she's worn ever since Harold met her at Mercer College so many years ago. Harold is sure she's wearing low heels and a shirtwaist dress. He knows her briefcase is in the backseat, containing lesson plans for today, yogurt, and a banana. Potassium is important. Harold has heard this a million times. Behind her, the beds are all made, the breakfast dishes stacked in the sink. As a home ec teacher, Joan believes that breakfast is the most important meal of the day. The two younger children, Brenda and Harold Jr., are already on the bus to the Academy. James rides to the high school with his mother, hair wet, face blank, staring straight ahead. They don't see Harold. Joan brakes at the stop sign before entering 15-501. She always comes to a complete stop, even if nothing's coming. Always. She looks both ways. Then she's gone.

Harold drives past well-kept lawn after well-kept lawn and lovely house after lovely house, many of them houses where Harold has attended Cub Scout meetings, eaten barbecue, watched bowl games. Now these houses have a blank, closed look to them, like mean faces. Harold turns left on Oxford, then right on Shrewsbury. He comes to a stop beside the curb at 1105 Cambridge and just sits there with the motor running, looking at the house. His house. The Queen Anne house he and Joan planned so carefully, down to the last detail, the fish-scale siding. The house he is still paying for and will be until his dying day, if Joan has her way about it.

Which she will, of course. Everybody is on her side: *desertion*. Harold Stikes deserted his lovely wife and three children for a redheaded waitress. For a fallen woman with a checkered past. Harold can hear her now. "I fail to see why I and the children should lower our standards of living, Harold, and go to the dogs just because you have chosen to become insane in mid-life." Joan's voice is slow and amiable. It has a down-to-earth quality which used to appeal to Harold but now drives him wild. Harold sits at the curb with the motor running and looks at his house good. It looks fine. It looks just like it did when they picked it out of the pages of *Southern Living* and wrote off for the plans. The only difference is, that house was in Stone Mountain, Georgia, and this house is in Greenwood, Mississippi. Big deal.

Joan's response to Harold's desertion has been a surprise to him. He expected tears, recriminations, fireworks. He did not expect her calm, reasonable manner, treating Harold the way she treats the Mormon missionaries who come to the door in their black suits, for instance, that very calm sweet careful voice. Joan acts like Harold's desertion is nothing much. And nothing much appears to have changed for her except the loss of Harold's actual presence, and this cannot be a very big deal since everything else has remained exactly the same.

What the hell. After a while Harold turns off the motor and walks up the flagstone walk to the front door. His key still fits. All the furniture is arranged exactly the way it was arranged four years ago. The only thing that ever changes here is the display of magazines on the glass coffee table before the fireplace, Joan keeps them up to date. *Newsweek, National Geographic, Good Housekeeping, Gourmet.* It's a mostly educational grouping, unlike what Cherry reads— *Parade, Coronet, National Enquirer.* Now these magazines litter the floor at the side of the bed like little souvenirs of Cherry. Harold can't stand to pick them up.

He sits down heavily on the white sofa and stares at the coffee table. He remembers the quiz and the day he found it, four years ago now although it feels like only yesterday, funny thing though that he can't remember which magazine it was in. Maybe *Reader's Digest.* The quiz was titled "How Good Is Your Marriage?" and Harold noticed that Joan had filled it in carefully. This did not surprise him. Joan was so law-abiding, such a *good girl*, that she always filled in such quizzes when she came across them, as if she *had to*, before she could go ahead and finish the magazine. Usually Harold didn't pay much attention.

This time, he picked the magazine up and started reading. One of the questions said: "What is your idea of the perfect vacation? (a) a romantic getaway for you and your spouse alone; (b) a family trip to the beach; (c) a business convention; (d) an organized tour of a foreign land." Joan had wavered on this one. She had marked and then erased "an organized tour of a foreign land." Finally she had settled on "a family trip to the beach." Harold skimmed along. The final question was: "When you think of the love between yourself and your spouse, do you think of (a) a great passion; (b) a warm, meaningful companionship; (c) an average love; (d) an unsatisfying habit." Joan had marked "(c) an average love." Harold stared at these words, knowing they were true. An average love, nothing great, an average marriage between an average man and woman. Suddenly, strangely, Harold was filled with rage.

"It is not enough!" He thought he actually said these words out loud. Perhaps he *did* say them out loud, into the clean hushed air-conditioned air of his average home. Harold's rage was followed by a brief period, maybe five minutes, of unbearable longing, after which he simply closed the magazine and put it back on the table and got up and poured himself a stiff shot of bourbon. He stood for a while before the picture window in the living room, looking out at his even green grass, his clipped hedge, and the impatiens blooming in its bed, the clematis climbing the mailbox. The colors of the world fairly leaped at him—the sky so blue, the grass so green. A passing jogger's shorts glowed unbearably red. He felt that he had never seen any of these things before. Yet in another way it all seemed so familiar as to be an actual part of his body—his throat, his heart, his breath. Harold took another drink. Then he went out and played nine holes of golf at the country club with Bubba Fields, something he did every Wednesday afternoon. He shot 82.

By the time he came home for dinner he was okay again. He was very tired and a little lightheaded, all his muscles tingling. His face was hot. Yet Harold felt vaguely pleased with himself, as if he had been through something and come out the other side of it, as if he had done a creditable job on a difficult assignment. But right then, during dinner, Harold could not have told you exactly what had happened to him that day, or why he felt this way. Because the mind will forget what it can't stand to remember, and anyway the Stikeses had beef Stroganoff that night, a new recipe that Joan was testing for the Junior League cookbook, and Harold Jr. had written them a funny letter from camp, and for once Brenda did not whine. James, who was twelve that year, actually condescended to talk to his father, with some degree of interest, about baseball, and after supper was over he and Harold went out and pitched to each other until it grew dark and lightning bugs emerged. This is how it's supposed to be, Harold thought, father and son playing catch in the twilight.

Then he went upstairs and joined Joan in bed to watch TV, after which they turned out the light and made love. But Joan had greased herself all over with Oil of Olay, earlier, and right in the middle of doing it, Harold got a crazy terrified feeling that he was losing her, that Joan was slipping, slipping away.

But time passed, as it does, and Harold forgot that whole weird day, forgot it until *right now*, in fact, as he sits on the white sofa in his old house again and stares at the magazines on the coffee table, those magazines so familiar except for the date, which is four years later. Now Harold wonders: If he hadn't picked up that quiz and read it, would he have even *noticed* when Cherry Oxendine spooned out that potato salad for him six months later, in his own Food Lion deli? Would the sight of redheaded Cherry Oxendine, the Food Lion smock mostly obscuring her dynamite figure, have hit him like a bolt out of the blue the way it did?

Cherry herself does not believe there is any such thing as coincidence. Cherry thinks there is a master plan for the universe, and what is *meant* to happen will. She thinks it's all set in the stars. For the first time, Harold thinks maybe she's right. He sees part of a pattern in the works, but dimly, as if he is looking at a constellation hidden by clouds. Mainly, he sees her face.

Harold gets up from the sofa and goes into the kitchen, suddenly aware that he isn't supposed to be here. He could be arrested, probably! He looks back at the living room but there's not a trace of him left, not even an imprint on the soft white cushions of the sofa. Absentmindedly, Harold opens and shuts the refrigerator door. There's no beer, he notices. He can't have a Coke. On the kitchen calendar, he reads:

Harold Jr to dentist, 3:30 p.m. Tues
Change furnace filter 2/18/88 (James)

So James is changing the furnace filters now, James is the man of the house. Why not? It's good for him. He's been given too much, kids these days grow up so fast, no responsibilities, they get on drugs, you read about it all the time. But deep down inside, Harold knows that James is not on drugs and he feels something awful, feels the way he felt growing up, that sick little flutter in his stomach that took years to go away.

Harold's dad died of walking pneumonia when he was only three, so his mother raised him alone. She called him her "little man." This made Harold feel proud but also wild, like a boy growing up in a cage. Does James feel this way now? Harold suddenly decides to get James a car for his birthday, and take him hunting.

Hunting is something Harold never did as a boy, but it means a lot to him now. In fact Harold never owned a gun until he was thirty-one, when he bought a shotgun in order to accept the invitation of his regional manager, "Little Jimmy" Fletcher, to go quail hunting in Georgia. He had a great time. Now he's invited back every year, and Little Jimmy is in charge of the company's whole eastern division. Harold has a great future with Food Lion too. He owns three stores, one in downtown Greenwood, one out at the mall, and one over in Indianola. He owned two of them when his mother died, and he's pleased to think that she died proud—proud of the good little boy he'd always been, and the good man he'd become.

Of course she'd wanted him to make a preacher, but Harold never got the call, and she gave that up finally when he was twenty. Harold was not going to pretend to get the call if he never got it, and he held strong to this principle.

He *wanted* to see a burning bush, but if this was not vouch-safed to him, he wasn't going to lie about it. He would just major in math instead, which he was good at anyway. Majoring in math at Mercer College, the small Baptist school his mother had chosen for him, Harold came upon Joan Berry, a home ec major from his own hometown who set out single-mindedly to marry him, which wasn't hard. After graduation, Harold got a job as management trainee in the Food Lion store where he had started as a bagboy at fourteen. Joan produced their three children, spaced three years apart, and got her tubes tied. Harold got one promotion, then another. Joan and Harold prospered. They built this house.

Harold looks around and now this house, his house, strikes him as creepy, a wax museum. He lets himself out the back door and walks quickly, almost runs, to his car. It's real cold out, a gray day in February, but Harold's sweating. He starts his car and roars off toward the hospital, driving—as Cherry would say—like a bat out of hell.

They're letting Harold stay with her longer now. He knows it, they know it, but nobody says a word. Lois Hickey just looks the other way when the announcement "Visiting hours are over" crackles across the PA. Is this a good sign or a bad sign? Harold can't tell. He feels slow and confused, like a man underwater. "I think she looks better, don't you?" he said last night to Cherry's son, Stan, the TV weatherman, who had driven down from Memphis for the day. Eyes slick and bright with tears, Stan went over to Harold and hugged him tight. This scared Harold to death, he has practically never touched his own sons, and he doesn't even *know* Stan, who's been grown and gone for years. Harold is not used to hugging anybody, especially men. Harold breathed in Stan's strong go-get-'em cologne, he buried his face in Stan's long curly hair. He thinks it is possible that Stan has a permanent. They'll do anything up in Memphis. Then Stan stepped back and put one hand on each of Harold's shoulders, holding him out at arm's length. Stan has his mother's wide, mobile mouth. The bright white light of Intensive Care glinted off the gold chain and the crystal that he wore around his neck. "I'm afraid we're going to lose her, Pop," he said.

But Harold doesn't think so. Today he thinks Cherry looks the best she's looked in weeks, with a bright spot of color in each cheek to match her flaming hair. She's moving around a lot too, she keeps kicking the sheet off.

"She's getting back some of that old energy now," he tells Cherry's daughter, Tammy Lynn Palladino, when she comes by after school. Tammy Lynn and Harold's son James are both members of the senior class, but they aren't friends. Tammy Lynn says James is a "stuck-up jock," a "preppie," and a "country-clubber." Harold can't say a word to defend his own son against these charges, he doesn't even *know* James anymore. It might be true, anyway. Tammy Lynn is real smart, a teenage egghead. She's got a full scholarship to Millsaps College for next year. She applied for it all by herself. As Cherry used to say, Tammy Lynn came into this world with a full deck of cards and an ace or two up her sleeve. Also she looks out for Number One.

In this regard Tammy Lynn is as different from her mama as night from day, because Cherry would give you the shirt off her back and frequently has. That's gotten her into lots of trouble. With Ed Palladino, for instance, her second husband and Tammy Lynn's dad. Just about everybody in this town got took by Ed Palladino, who came in here wearing a seersucker suit and talking big about putting in an outlet mall across the river. A lot of people got burned on that outlet mall deal. But Ed Palladino had a way about him that made you want to cast your lot with his, it is true. You wanted to give Ed Palladino your savings, your timesharing condo, your cousin, your ticket to the Super Bowl. Cherry gave it all.

She married him and turned over what little inheritance she had from her daddy's death—and that's the only time in her life she ever had *any* money, mind you—and then she just shrugged and smiled her big crooked smile when he left town under cover of night. *"C'est la vie,"* Cherry said. She donated the rest of his clothes to the Salvation Army. *"Que será, será,"* Cherry said, quoting a song that was popular when she was in junior high.

Tammy Lynn sits by her mama's bed and holds Cherry's thin dry hand. "I brought you a Chick-Fil-A," she says to

Harold. "It's over there in that bag." She points to the shelf
by the door. Harold nods. Tammy Lynn works at Chick-
Fil-A. Cherry's eyes are wide and blue and full of meaning
as she stares at her daughter. Her mouth moves, both Harold and Tammy Lynn lean forward, but then her mouth
falls slack and her eyelids flutter shut. Tammy sits back.

"I think she looks some better today, don't you?" Harold
asks.

"No," Tammy Lynn says. She has a flat little redneck
voice. She sounds just the way she did last summer when
she told Cherry that what she saw in the field was a cotton
picker working at night, and not a UFO after all. "I wish
I did but I don't, Harold. I'm going to go on home now and
heat up some Beanee Weenee for Mamaw. You come on as
soon as you can."

"Well," Harold says. He feels like things have gotten all
turned around here some way, he feels like he's the kid and
Tammy Lynn has turned into a freaky little grown-up. He
says, "I'll be along directly."

But they both know he won't leave until Lois Hickey
throws him out. And speaking of Lois, as soon as Tammy
Lynn takes off, here she comes again, checking something
on the respirator, making a little clucking sound with her
mouth, then whirling to leave. When Lois walks, her panty
girdle goes *swish, swish, swish* at the top of her legs. She
comes right back with the young black man named Rodney
Broadbent, Respiratory Therapist. It says so on his badge.

Rodney wheels a complicated-looking cart ahead of himself. He's all built up, like a weightlifter.

"How you doing tonight, Mr. Stipe?" Rodney says.

"I think she's some better," Harold says.

Lois Hickey and Rodney look at him.

"Well, lessee here," Rodney says. He unhooks the respirator tube at Cherry's throat, sticks the tube from his own machine down the opening, and switches on the machine. It makes a whirring sound. It looks like an electric ice cream mixer. Rodney Broadbent looks at Lois Hickey in a significant way as she turns to leave the room.

They don't have to tell him, Harold knows. Cherry is worse, not better. Harold gets the Chick-Fil-A, unwraps it, eats it, and then goes over to stand by the window. It's already getting dark. The big mercury arc light glows in the hospital parking lot. A little wind blows some trash around on the concrete. He has had Cherry for three years, that's all. One trip to Disney World, two vacations at Gulf Shores Alabama, hundreds of nights in the old metal bed out at the farm with Cherry sleeping naked beside him, her arm thrown over his stomach. They had a million laughs.

"Alrightee," Rodney Broadbent nearly sings, unhooking his machine. Harold turns to look at him. Rodney Broadbent certainly looks more like a middle linebacker than a respiratory therapist. But Harold likes him.

"Well, Rodney?" Harold says.

Rodney starts shadow-boxing in the middle of the room. "Tough times," he says finally. "These is tough times,

Mr. Stipe." Harold stares at him. Rodney is light on his feet as can be.

Harold sits down in the chair by the respirator. "What do you mean?" he asks.

"I mean she is drowning, Mr. Stipe," Rodney says. He throws a punch which lands real close to Harold's left ear. "What I'm doing here, see, is suctioning. I'm pulling all the fluid up out of her lungs. But now looka here, Mr. Stipe, they is just too damn much of it. See this little doohickey here I'm measuring it with? This here is the danger zone, man. Now Mrs. Stipe, she has been in the danger zone for some time. They is just too much damn fluid in there. What she got, anyway? Cancer and pneumonia both, am I right? What can I tell you, man? She is *drowning.*" Rodney gives Harold a short affectionate punch in the ribs, then wheels his cart away. From the door, apparently struck by some misgivings, he says, "Well, man, if it was me, I'd want to know what the story is, you follow me, man? If it was me, what I'm saying." Harold can't see Rodney anymore, only hear his voice from the open door.

"Thank you, Rodney," Harold says. He sits in the chair. In a way he has known this already, for quite some time. In a way, Rodney's news is no news, to Harold. He just hopes he will be man enough to bear it, to do what will have to be done. Harold has always been scared that he is not man enough for Cherry Oxendine, anyway. This is his worst secret fear. He looks around the little Intensive Care room, searching for a sign, some sign, anything, that he will be man enough. Nothing happens. Cherry lies strapped to the bed, flanked by so many machines that it looks like she's in the cockpit of a jet. Her eyes are closed, eyelids fluttering, red spots on her freckled cheeks. Her chest rises and falls as the respirator pushes air in and out through the tube in her neck. He doesn't see how she can sleep in the bright white light of Intensive Care, where it is always noon. And does she dream? Cherry used to tell him her dreams, which were wild, long Technicolor dreams, like movies. Cherry played different parts in them. If you dream in color, it means you're intelligent, Cherry said. She used to tease him all the time. She thought Harold's own dreams were a stitch, dreams more boring than his life, dreams in which he'd drive to Jackson, say, or be washing his car.

"Harold?" It's Ray Muncey, manager of the Food Lion at the mall.

"Why, what are you doing over here, Ray?" Harold asks, and then in a flash he *knows*, Lois Hickey must have called him, to make Harold go on home.

"I was just driving by and I thought, Hey, maybe Harold and me might run by the Holiday Inn, get a bite to eat." Ray shifts from foot to foot in the doorway. He doesn't come inside, he's not supposed to, nobody but immediate family is allowed in Intensive Care, and Harold's glad— Cherry would just die if people she barely knows, like Ray Muncey, got to see her looking so bad.

"No, Ray, you go on and eat," Harold says. "I already ate. I'm leaving right now, anyway."

"Well, how's the missus doing?" Ray is a big man, afflicted with big, heavy manners.

"She's drowning," Harold says abruptly. Suddenly he remembers Cherry in a water ballet at the town pool, it must have been the summer of junior year, Fourth of July, Cherry and the other girls floating in a circle on their backs to form a giant flower—legs high, toes pointed. Harold doesn't know it when Ray Muncey leaves. Out the window, the parking lot light glows like a big full moon. Lois Hickey comes in. "You've got to go home now, Harold," she says. "I'll call if there's any change." He remembers Cherry at Glass Lake, on the senior class picnic. Cherry's getting real agitated now, she tosses her head back and forth, moves her arms. She'd pull out the tubes if she could. She kicks off the sheet. Her legs are still good, great legs in fact, the legs of a beautiful young woman.

Harold at seventeen was tall and skinny, brown hair in a soft flat crew cut, glasses with heavy black frames. His jeans were too short. He carried a pen-and-pencil set in a clear plastic case in his breast pocket. Harold and his best friend, Ben Hill, looked so much alike that people had trouble telling them apart. They did everything together. They built model rockets, they read every science fiction book they could get their hands on, they collected Lionel train parts and Marvel comics. They loved superheroes with special powers, enormous beings who leaped across rivers and oceans. Harold's friendship with Ben Hill kept the awful loneliness of the only child at bay, and it also kept him from having to talk to girls. You couldn't talk to those two, not seriously. They were giggling and bumping into each other all the time. They were immature.

So it was in Ben's company that Harold experienced the most private, the most *personal* memory he has of Cherry Oxendine in high school. Oh, he also has those other memories you'd expect, the big public memories of Cherry being crowned Miss Greenwood High (for her talent; she surprised everybody by reciting "Abou Ben Adhem" in such a stirring way that there wasn't a dry eye in the whole auditorium when she got through), or running out onto the field ahead of the team with the other cheerleaders, red curls flying, green and white skirt whirling out around her hips like a beach umbrella when she turned a cartwheel. Harold noticed her then, of course. He noticed her when she moved through the crowded halls of the high school with her walk that was almost a prance, she put a little something extra into it, all right. Harold noticed Cherry Oxendine then in the way that he noticed Sandra Dee on the cover of a magazine, or Annette Funicello on *American Bandstand.*

But such girls were not for the likes of Harold, and Harold knew it. Girls like Cherry always had boyfriends like Lamar Peebles, who was hers—a doctor's son with a baby-blue convertible and plenty of money. They used to drive around town in his car, smoking cigarettes. Harold saw them, as he carried out grocery bags. He did not envy Lamar Peebles, or wish he had a girl like Cherry Oxendine. Only something about them made him stand where he was in the Food Lion lot, watching, until they had passed from sight.

So Harold's close-up encounter with Cherry was unexpected. It took place at the senior class picnic, where Harold and Ben had been drinking beer all afternoon. No alcohol was allowed at the senior class picnic, but some of the more enterprising boys had brought out kegs the night before and hidden them in the woods. Anybody could go back there and pay some money and get some beer. The chaperones didn't know, or appeared not to know. In any case, the chaperones all left at six o'clock, when the picnic was officially over. Some of the class members left then too. Then some of them came back with more beer, more blankets. It was a free lake. Nobody could *make* you go home. Normally, Harold and Ben would have been among the first to leave, but because they had had four beers apiece, and because this was the first time they had ever had *any* beer ever, at all, they were still down by the water, skipping rocks and waiting to sober up so that they would not wreck Harold's mother's green Gremlin on the way home. All the cool kids were on the other side of the lake, listening to transistor radios. The sun went down. Bullfrogs started up. A mist came out all around the sides of the lake. It was a cloudy, humid day anyway, not a great day for a picnic.

"If God is really God, how come He let Himself get crucified, is what I want to know," Ben said. Ben's daddy was a Holiness preacher, out in the county.

But Harold heard something. "Hush, Ben," he said.

"If I was God I would go around and really kick some ass," Ben said.

Harold heard it again. It was almost too dark to see.

"Damn." It was a girl's voice, followed by a splash.

All of a sudden, Harold felt sober. "Who's there?" he asked. He stepped forward, right up to the water's edge. Somebody was in the water. Harold was wearing his swim trunks under his jeans, but he had not gone in the water himself. He couldn't stand to show himself in front of people. He thought he was too skinny.

"Well, *do something.*" It was the voice of Cherry Oxendine, almost wailing. She stumbled up the bank. Harold reached out and grabbed her arm. Close up, she was a mess, wet and muddy, with her hair all over her head. But the thing that got Harold, of course, was that she didn't have any top on. She didn't even try to cover them up either, just stomped her little foot on the bank and said, "I am going to *kill* Lamar Peebles when I get ahold of him." Harold had never even imagined so much skin.

"What's going on?" asked Ben, from up the bank.

Harold took off his own shirt as fast as he could and handed it over to Cherry Oxendine. "Cover yourself," he said.

"Why, thank you." Cherry didn't bat an eye. She took

his shirt and put it on, tying it stylishly at the waist. Harold couldn't believe it. Close up, Cherry was a lot smaller than she looked on the stage or the football field. She looked up at Harold through her dripping hair and gave him her crooked grin.

"Thanks, hey?" she said.

And then she was gone, vanished into the mist and trees before Harold could say another word. He opened his mouth and closed it. Mist obscured his view. From the other side of the lake he could hear "Ramblin' Rose" playing on somebody's radio. He heard a girl's high-pitched giggle, a boy's whooping laugh.

"What's going on?" asked Ben.

"Nothing," Harold said. It was the first time he had ever lied to Ben. Harold never told anybody what had happened that night, not ever. He felt that it was up to him to protect Cherry Oxendine's honor. Later, much later, when he and Cherry were lovers, he was astonished to learn that she couldn't remember any of this, not who she was with or what had happened or what she was doing in the lake like that with her top off, or Harold giving her his shirt. "I think that was sweet, though," Cherry told him.

When Harold and Ben finally got home that night at nine or ten o'clock, Harold's mother was frantic. "You've been drinking," she shrilled at him under the hanging porch light. "And where's your shirt?" It was a new madras shirt which Harold had gotten for graduation. Now Harold's mother is out at the Hillandale Rest Home. Ben died in Vietnam, and Cherry is drowning. This time, and Harold knows it now, he can't help her.

Oh, Cherry! Would she have been so wild if she hadn't been so cute? And what if her parents had been younger when she was born—normal-age parents—couldn't they have controlled her better? As it was, the Oxendines were sober, solid people living in a farmhouse out near the county line, and Cherry lit up their lives like a rocket. Her dad, Martin "Buddy" Oxendine, went to sleep in his chair every night right after supper, woke back up for the eleven o'clock news, and then went to bed for good. Buddy was an elder in the Baptist church. Cherry's mom, Gladys Oxendine, made drapes for people. She assumed she would never have children at all because of her spastic colitis. Gladys and Buddy had started raising cockapoos when they gave up on children. Imagine Gladys's surprise, then, to find herself pregnant at thirty-eight, when she was already old! They say she didn't even know it when she went to the doctor. She thought she had a tumor.

But then she got so excited, that old farm woman, when Dr. Grimwood told her what was what, and she wouldn't even consider an abortion when he mentioned the chances of a mongoloid. People didn't use to have babies so old then as they do now, so Gladys Oxendine's pregnancy was the talk of the county. Neighbors crocheted little jackets and made receiving blankets. Buddy built a baby room onto the house and made a cradle by hand. During the last two months of the pregnancy, when Gladys had to stay in bed because of toxemia, people brought over casseroles and boiled custard, everything good. Gladys's pregnancy was the only time in her whole life that she was ever pretty, and she loved it, and she loved the attention, neighbors in and out of the house. When the baby was finally born on November 1, 1944, no parents were ever more ready than Gladys and Buddy Oxendine. And the baby was everything they hoped for too, which is not usually the case—the prettiest baby in the world, a baby like a little flower.

They named her Doris Christine which is who she was until eighth grade, when she made junior varsity cheerleader and announced that she was changing her name to Cherry. Cherry! Even her parents had to admit it suited her better than Doris Christine. As a little girl, Doris Christine was redheaded, bouncy, and busy—she was always into something, usually something you'd never thought to tell her not to do. She started talking early and never shut up. Her old dad, old Buddy Oxendine, was so crazy about Doris Christine that he took her everywhere with him in his red pickup truck. You got used to seeing the two of them, Buddy and his curly-headed little daughter, riding the country roads together, going to the seed-and-feed together, sharing a shake at the Dairy Queen. Gladys made all of Doris Christine's clothes, the most beautiful little dresses in the world, with hand-smocking and French seams. They gave Doris Christine everything they could think of—what she asked for, what she didn't. "That child is going to get spoiled," people started to say. And of course she did get spoiled, she couldn't have helped *that*, but she was never spoiled rotten as so many are. She stayed sweet in spite of it all.

Then along about ninth grade, soon after she changed her name to Cherry and got interested in boys, things changed between Cherry and the old Oxendines. Stuff happened. Instead of being the light of their lives, Cherry became the bane of their existence, the curse of their old age. She wanted to wear makeup, she wanted to have car dates. You can't blame her—she was old enough, sixteen. Everybody else did it. But you can't blame Gladys and Buddy either—they were old people by then, all worn out. They were not up to such a daughter. Cherry sneaked out. She wrecked a car. She ran away to Pensacola with a soldier. Finally, Gladys and Buddy just gave up. When Cherry eloped with the disc jockey, Don Westall, right after graduation, they threw up their hands. They did not do a thing about it. They had done the best they could, and everybody knew it. They went back to raising cockapoos.

Cherry, living up in Nashville, Tennessee, had a baby, Stan, the one that's in his twenties now. Cherry sent baby pictures back to Gladys and Buddy, and wrote that she was going to be a singer. Six years later, she came home. She said nothing against Don Westall, who was still a disc jockey on WKIX, Nashville. You could hear him on the radio every night after ten P.M. Cherry said the breakup was all her fault. She said she had made some mistakes, but she didn't say what they were. She was thin and noble. Her kid was cute. She did not go back out to the farm then. She rented an apartment over the hardware store, down by the river, and got a job downtown working in Ginger's Boutique. After a year or so, she started acting more like herself again, although not *quite* like herself, she had grown up somehow in Nashville, and quit being spoiled. She put Stan, her kid, first. And if she did run around a little bit, or if she was the life of the party sometimes out at the country club, so what? Stan didn't want for a thing. By then the Oxendines were failing and she had to take care of them too, she had to drive her daddy up to Grenada for dialysis twice a week. It was not an easy life for Cherry, but if it ever got her down, you couldn't tell it. She was still cute. When her daddy finally died and left her a little money, everybody was real glad. Oh *now*, they said, Cherry Oxendine can quit working so hard and put her mama in a home or something and have a decent life. She can go on a cruise. But then along came Ed Palladino, and the rest is history.

Cherry Oxendine was left with no husband, no money, a little girl, and a mean old mama to take care of. At least by this time Stan was in the Navy. Cherry never complained, though. She moved back out to the farm. When Ginger retired from business and closed her boutique, Cherry got another job, as a receptionist at Wallace, Wallace and Peebles. This was her undoing. Because Lamar Peebles had just moved back to town with his family, to join his father's firm. Lamar had two little girls. He had been married to a tobacco heiress since college. All this time he had run around on her. He was not on the up-and-up. And when he encountered redheaded Cherry Oxendine again after the passage of so many years, all those old fireworks went off again. They got to be a scandal, then a disgrace. Lamar said he was going to marry her, and Cherry believed him. After six months of it, Mrs. Lamar Peebles checked herself into a mental hospital in Silver Hill, Connecticut. First, she called her lawyers.

And then it was all over, not even a year after it began. Mr. and Mrs. Lamar Peebles were reconciled and moved to Winston-Salem, North Carolina, her hometown. Cherry Oxendine lost her job at Wallace, Wallace and Peebles, and was reduced to working in the deli at Food Lion. Why did she do it? Why did she lose all the goodwill she'd built up in this community over so many years? It is because she doesn't know how to look out for Number One. Her own daughter, Tammy Lynn Palladino, is aware of this.

"You have got a fatal flaw, Mama," Tammy said after learning about fatal flaws in English class. "You believe everything everybody tells you."

Still, Tammy loves her mother. Sometimes she writes her mother's whole name, Cherry Oxendine Westall Palladino Stikes, over and over in her Blue Horse notebook. Tammy Lynn will never be half the woman her mother is, and she's so smart she knows it. She gets a kick out of her mother's wild ideas.

"When you get too old to be cute, honey, you get to be eccentric," Cherry told Tammy one time. It's the truest thing she ever said.

It seems to Tammy that the main thing about her mother is, Cherry always has to have *something* going on. If it isn't a man it's something else, such as having her palm read by that woman over in French Camp, or astrology, or the grapefruit diet. Cherry believes in the Bermuda Triangle, Bigfoot, Atlantis, and ghosts. It kills her that she's not psychic. The UFO Club was just the latest in a long string of interests although it has lasted the longest, starting back before Cherry's marriage to Harold Stikes. And then Cherry got cancer, and she kind of forgot about it. But Tammy still remembers the night her mama first got so turned on to UFOs.

Rhonda Ramey, Cherry's best friend, joined the UFO Club first. Rhonda and Cherry are a lot alike, although it's hard to see this at first. While Cherry is short and peppy, Rhonda is tall, thin, and listless. She looks like Cher. Rhonda doesn't have any children. She's crazy about her husband, Bill, but he's a workaholic who runs a string of video rental stores all over northern Mississippi, so he's gone a lot, and Rhonda gets bored. She works out at the spa, but it isn't enough. Maybe this is why she got so interested when the UFO landed at a farm outside her mother's hometown of Como. It was first spotted by sixteen-year-old

Donnie Johnson just at sunset, as he was finishing his chores on his parents' farm. He heard a loud rumbling sound "in the direction of the hog house," it said in the paper. Looking up, he suddenly saw a "brilliantly lit mushroom-shaped object" hovering about two feet above the ground, with a shaft of white light below and glowing all over with an intensely bright multicolored light, "like the light of a welder's arc."

Donnie said it sounded like a jet. He was temporarily blinded and paralyzed. He fell down on the ground. When he came back to his senses again, it was gone. Donnie staggered into the kitchen where his parents, Durel, fifty-four, and Erma, forty-nine, were eating supper, and told them what had happened. They all ran back outside to the field, where they found four large imprints and four small imprints in the muddy ground, and a nearby clump of sage grass on fire. The hogs were acting funny, bunching up, looking dazed. Immediately, Durel jumped in his truck and went to get the sheriff, who came right back with two deputies. All in all, six people viewed the site while the bush continued to burn, and who knows how many people—half of Como—saw the imprints the next day. Rhonda saw them too. She drove out to the Johnson farm with her mother, as soon as she heard about it.

It was a close encounter of the second kind, according to Civil Air Patrol head Glenn Raines, who appeared on TV to discuss it, because the UFO "interacted with its surroundings in a significant way." A close encounter of the first kind is simply a close-range sighting, while a close encounter of the third kind is something like the most famous example, of Betty and Barney Hill of Exeter, New Hampshire, who were actually kidnapped by a UFO while they were driving along on a trip. Betty and Barney Hill were taken aboard the alien ship and given physical exams by intelligent humanoid beings. Two hours and thirty-five minutes were missing from their trip, and afterward, Betty had to be treated for acute anxiety. Glenn Raines, wearing his brown Civil Air Patrol uniform, said all this on TV.

His appearance, plus what had happened at the Johnson farm, sparked a rash of sightings all across Mississippi, Louisiana, and Texas for the next two years. Metal disk-like objects were seen, and luminous objects appearing as lights at night. In Levelland, Texas, fifteen people called the police to report an egg-shaped UFO appearing over State Road 1173. Overall, the UFOs seemed to show a preference for soybean fields and teenage girl viewers. But a pretty good photograph of a UFO flying over the Gulf was taken by a retired man from Pascagoula, so you can't generalize. Clubs sprang up all over the place. The one that Rhonda and Cherry went to had seventeen members and met once a month at the junior high school.

Tammy recalls exactly how her mama and Rhonda acted the night they came home from Cherry's first meeting. Cherry's eyes sparkled in her face like Brenda Starr's eyes in the comics. She started right in telling Tammy all about it, beginning with the Johnsons from Como and Betty and Barney Hill.

Tammy was not impressed. "I don't believe it," she said. She was president of the Science Club at the junior high school.

"You are the most irritating child!" Cherry said. "*What* don't you believe?"

"Well, any of it," Tammy said then. "All of it," and this has remained her attitude ever since.

"Listen, honey, *Jimmy Carter* saw one," Cherry said triumphantly. "In nineteen seventy-one, at the Executive Mansion in Georgia. He turned in an official report on it."

"How come nobody knows about it, then?" Tammy asked. She was a tough customer.

"Because the government covered it up!" said Rhonda, just dying to tell this part. "People see UFOs all the time, it's common knowledge, they are trying to make contact with us right now, honey, but the government doesn't want the average citizen to know about it. There's a big cover-up going on."

"It's just like Watergate." Cherry opened a beer and handed it over to Rhonda.

"That's right," Rhonda said, "and every time there's a major incident, you know what happens? These men from the government show up at your front door dressed all in black. After they get through with you, you'll wish you never heard the word 'saucer.' You turn pale and get real sick. You can't get anything to stay on your stomach."

Tammy cracked up. But Rhonda and Cherry went on and on. They had official-looking gray notebooks to log their sightings in. At their meetings, they reported these sightings to each other, and studied up on the subject in general. Somebody in the club was responsible for the educational part of each meeting, and somebody else brought the refreshments.

Tammy Lynn learned to keep her mouth shut. It was less embarrassing than belly dancing; she had a friend whose mother took belly dancing at the YMCA. Tammy did not tell her mama about all the rational explanations for UFOs that she found in the school library. They included: (1) hoaxes; (2) natural phenomena, such as fungus causing the so-called fairy rings sometimes found after a landing; (3) real airplanes flying off course; and Tammy's favorite, (4) the Fata Morgana, described as a "rare and beautiful type of mirage, constantly changing, the result of unstable layers of warm and cold air. The Fata Morgana takes its name from fairy lore and is said to evoke in the viewer a profound sense of longing," the book went on to say. Tammy's biology teacher, Mr. Owens, said he thought that the weather patterns in Mississippi might be especially conducive to this phenomenon. But Tammy kept her mouth shut. And after a while, when nobody in the UFO Club saw anything, its membership declined sharply. Then her mama met Harold Stikes, then Harold Stikes left his wife and children and moved out to the farm with them, and sometimes Cherry forgot to attend the meetings, she was so happy with Harold Stikes.

Tammy couldn't see *why*, initially. In her opinion, Harold Stikes was about as interesting as a telephone pole. "But he's so *nice!*" Cherry tried to explain it to Tammy Lynn. Finally Tammy decided that there is nothing in the world that makes somebody as attractive as if they really love you. And Harold Stikes really did love her mama, there was no question. That old man—what a crazy old Romeo! Why, he proposed to Cherry when she was still in the hospital after she had her breast removed (this was back when they thought that was *it*, that the doctors had gotten it all).

"Listen, Cherry," he said solemnly, gripping a dozen red roses. "I want you to marry me."

"What?" Cherry said. She was still groggy.

"I want you to marry me," Harold said. He knelt down heavily beside her bed.

"Harold! Get up from there!" Cherry said. "Somebody will see you."

"Say yes," said Harold.

"I just had my breast removed."

"Say yes," he said again.

"*Yes, yes, yes!*" Cherry said.

And as soon as she got out of the hospital, they were married out in the orchard, on a beautiful April day, by Lew Uggams, a JP from out of town. They couldn't find a local preacher to do it. The sky was bright blue, not a cloud in sight. Nobody was invited except Stan, Tammy, Rhonda and Bill, and Cherry's mother, who wore her dress inside out. Cherry wore a new pink lace dress, the color of cherry blossoms. Tough little Tammy cried and cried. It's the most beautiful wedding she's ever seen, and now she's completely devoted to Harold Stikes.

So Tammy leaves the lights on for Harold when she finally goes to bed that night. She tried to wait up for him, but she has to go to school in the morning, she's got a chemistry test. Her mamaw is sound asleep in the little added-on baby room that Buddy Oxendine built for Cherry. Gladys acts like a baby now, a spoiled baby at that. The only thing she'll drink is Sprite out of a can. She talks mean. She doesn't like anything in the world except George and Tammy, the two remaining cockapoos.

They bark up a storm when Harold finally gets back out to the farm, at one-thirty. The cockapoos are barking, Cherry's mom is snoring like a chain saw. Harold doesn't see how Tammy Lynn can sleep through all of this, but she always does. Teenagers can sleep through anything. Harold himself has started waking up several times a night, his heart pounding. He wonders if he's going to have a heart attack. He almost mentioned his symptoms to Lois Hickey last week, in fact, but then thought, What the hell. His heart is broken. Of course it's going to act up some.

And everything, not only his heart, is out of whack. Sometimes he'll break into a sweat for no reason. Often he forgets really crucial things, such as filing his estimated income tax on January 15. Harold is not the kind to forget something this important. He has strange aches that float from joint to joint. He has headaches. He's lost twelve pounds. Sometimes he has no appetite at all. Other times, like right now, he's just starving.

Harold goes in the kitchen and finds a flat rectangular casserole, carefully wrapped in tinfoil, on the counter, along with a Tupperware cake carrier. He lifts off the top of the cake carrier and finds a piña colada cake, his favorite. Then he pulls back the tinfoil on the casserole. Lasagna! Plenty is left over. Harold sticks it in the microwave. He knows that the cake and the lasagna were left here by his ex-wife. Ever since Cherry has been in Intensive Care, Joan has been bringing food out to the farm. She comes when Harold's at work or at the hospital, and leaves it with Gladys or Tammy. She probably figures that Harold would refuse it, if she caught him at home, which he would. She's a great cook, though. Harold takes the lasagna out of the microwave, opens a beer, and sits down at the kitchen table. He loves Joan's lasagna. Cherry's idea of a terrific meal is one she doesn't have to cook. Harold remembers eating in bed with Cherry, tacos from Taco Bell, sour-cream-and-onion chips, beer. He gets some more lasagna and a big wedge of piña colada cake.

Now it's two-thirty, but for some reason Harold is not a bit sleepy. His mind whirls with thoughts of Cherry. He snaps off all the lights and stands in the darkened house. His heart is racing. Moonlight comes in the windows, it falls on the old patterned rug. Outside, it's as bright as day. He puts his coat on and goes out, with the cockapoos scampering along beside him. They are not even surprised. They think it's a fine time for a walk. Harold goes past the mailbox, down the dirt road between the fields. Out here in the country, the sky is both bigger and closer than it is in town. Harold feels like he's in a huge bowl turned upside down, with tiny little pinpoints of light shining through. And everything is silvered by the moonlight—the old fence posts, the corn stubble in the flat long fields, a distant barn, the highway at the end of the dirt road, his own strange hand when he holds it out to look at it.

He remembers when she waited on him in the Food Lion deli, three years ago. He had asked for a roast beef sandwich, which come prepackaged. Cherry put it on his plate. Then she paused, and cocked her hip, and looked at him. "Can I give you some potato salad to go with that?" she asked. "Some slaw?"

Harold looked at her. Some red curls had escaped the required net. "Nothing else," he said.

But Cherry spooned a generous helping of potato salad onto his plate. "Thank you so much," he said. They looked at each other.

"I know I know you," Cherry said.

It came to him then. "Cherry Oxendine," said Harold. "I remember you from high school."

"Lord, you've got a great memory, then!" Cherry had an easy laugh. "That was a hundred years ago."

"Doesn't seem like it." Harold knew he was holding up the line.

"Depends on who you're talking to," Cherry said.

Later that day, Harold found an excuse to go back over to the deli for coffee and apple pie, then he found an excuse to look through the personnel files. He started eating lunch at the deli every day, without making any conscious decision to do so. In the afternoons, when he went back for coffee, Cherry would take her break and sit at a table with him.

Harold and Cherry talked and talked. They talked about their families, their kids, high school. Cherry told him everything that had happened to her. She was tough and funny, not bitter or self-pitying. They talked and talked. In his whole life, Harold had never had so much to say. During this period, which lasted for several weeks, his whole life took on a heightened aspect. Everything that happened to him seemed significant, a little incident to tell Cherry about. Every song he liked on the radio he remembered, so he could ask Cherry if she liked it too. Then there came the day when they were having coffee and she mentioned she'd left her car at Al's Garage that morning to get a new clutch.

"I'll give you a ride over there to pick it up," said Harold instantly. In his mind he immediately canceled the sales meeting he had scheduled for four o'clock.

"Oh, that's too much trouble," Cherry said.

"But I insist." In his conversations with Cherry, Harold had developed a brand-new gallant manner he had never had before.

"Well, if you're sure it's not any trouble . . ." Cherry grinned at him like she knew he really wanted to do it, and that afternoon when he grabbed her hand suddenly before letting her out at Al's Garage, she did not pull it away.

The next weekend Harold took her up to Memphis and they stayed at the Peabody Hotel, where Cherry got the biggest kick out of the ducks in the lobby, and ordering from room service.

"You're a fool," Harold's friends told him later, when the shit hit the fan.

But Harold didn't think so. He doesn't think so now, walking the old dirt road on the Oxendine farm in the moonlight. He loves his wife. He feels that he has been ennobled and enlarged, by knowing Cherry Oxendine. He feels like he has been specially selected among men, to receive a precious gift. He stepped out of his average life for her, he gave up being a good man, but the rewards have been extraordinary. He's glad he did it. He'd do it all over again.

Still walking, Harold suddenly knows that something is going to happen. But he doesn't stop walking. Only, the whole world around him seems to waver a bit, and intensify.

The moonlight shines whiter than ever. A little wind whips up out of nowhere. The stars are twinkling so brightly that they seem to dance, actually dance, in the sky. And then, while Harold watches, one of them detaches itself from the rest of the sky and grows larger, moves closer, until it's clear that it is actually moving across the sky, at an angle to the earth. A falling star, perhaps? A comet?

Harold stops walking. The star moves faster and faster, with an erratic pattern. It's getting real close now. It's no star. Harold hears a high whining noise, like a blender. The cockapoos huddle against his ankles. They don't bark. Now he can see the blinking red lights on the top of it, and the beam of white light shooting out the bottom. His coat is blown straight out behind him by the wind. He feels like he's going blind. He shields his eyes. At first it's as big as a barn, then a tobacco warehouse. It covers the field. Although Harold can't say exactly how it communicates to him or even if it does, suddenly his soul is filled to bursting. The ineffable occurs. And then, more quickly than it came, it's gone, off toward Carrollton, rising into the night, leaving the field, the farm, the road. Harold turns back.

It will take Cherry Oxendine two more weeks to die. She's tough. And even when there's nothing left of her but heart, she will fight all the way. She will go out furious, squeezing Harold's hand at the very moment of death, clinging fast to every minute of this bright, hard life. And although at first he won't want to, Harold will go on living.

He will buy another store. Gladys will die. Tammy Lynn will make Phi Beta Kappa. Harold will start attending the Presbyterian church again. Eventually Harold may even go back to his family, but he will love Cherry Oxendine until the day he dies, and he will never, ever, tell anybody what he saw.

Me and My Baby
View the Eclipse

Sharon Shaw first met her lover, Raymond Stewart, in an incident that took place in broad daylight at the Xerox machine in Stewart's Pharmacy three years ago—it *can't* be that long! Sharon just can't believe it. Every time she thinks about him now, no matter what she's doing, she stops right in the middle of it while a hot crazy ripple runs over her entire body. This makes her feel like she's going to die or throw up. Of course she never does either one. She pats her hair and goes right on with her busy life the way she did *before* she met him, but everything is different now, all altered, all new. Three years! Her children were little then: Leonard Lee was eleven, Alister was ten, and Margaret, the baby, was only three. Sharon was thirty-four. Now she's over the hill, but who cares? Since the children are all in school, she and Raymond can meet more easily.

"Is the *coast clear?*" Raymond will ask with his high nervous giggle, at her back door. Raymond speaks dramatically, emphasizing certain words. He flings his arms around. He wears huge silky handkerchiefs and gold neck-chains and drives all the way to Roanoke to get his hair cut in what he calls a modified punk look. In fact Raymond is a figure of fun in Roxboro, which Sharon knows, and this knowledge just about kills her. She wants to grab him up and soothe him, smooth down his bristling blond hair and press his fast-beating little heart against her deep soft bosom and wrap him around and around in her big strong arms. Often, she does this. "Hush now, honey," she says.

For Raymond is misunderstood. Roxboro is divided into two camps about him, the ones who call him Raymond, which is his name, and the ones who call him Ramón, with the accent on the last syllable, which is what he *wants* to be called. "Putting on airs just like his daddy did," sniffs Sharon's mama, who works at the courthouse and knows everything. Raymond's daddy was a pharmacist who, according to Sharon's mama, never got over not being a doctor. She says this is common among pharmacists. She says he was a dope fiend too. Sharon doesn't know if this part is true or not, and she won't ask; the subject of his father—who killed himself—gives Raymond nervous palpitations of the heart. Anyway this is how Raymond came to be working at Stewart's Pharmacy, where he mostly runs the Xerox machine and helps ladies order stationery and wedding invitations from huge bound books which he keeps on a round coffee table in his conversation area—Raymond likes for things to be nice. A tall, sour-faced man named Mr. Gardiner is the actual manager—everybody knows that Raymond could never run a store. Raymond stays busy, though. He does brochures and fliers and handouts, whatever you want, on his big humming Xerox machine, and he'll give you a cup of coffee to drink while you make up your mind. This coffee is strong, sweet stuff. Sharon had never tasted anything quite like it before the day she went in there to discuss how much it would cost to print up a little cookbook of everybody's favorite recipes from the Shady Mountain Elementary School PTA to make extra money for art.

It was late August, hot as blazes outside, so it took Sharon just a minute to recover from the heat. She's a large, slow-moving woman anyway, with dark brown eyes and dark brown hair and bright deep color in her cheeks. She has what her mother always called a "peaches-'n'-cream complexion." She used to hear her mother saying that on the phone to her Aunt Marge, talking about Sharon's "peaches-'n'-cream complexion" and about how she was so "slow," and wouldn't "stand up for herself." This meant going out for cheerleader. Later, these conversations were all about how Sharon would never "live up to her potential," which meant marrying a doctor, a potential that went up in smoke the day Sharon announced that she was going to marry Leonard Shaw, her high school sweetheart, after all.

Now Sharon talks to her mother every day on the

telephone, unless of course she sees her, and her mother still talks every day to Sharon's Aunt Marge. Sharon has worn her pretty hair in the same low ponytail ever since high school, which doesn't seem so long ago to her either. It seems like yesterday, in fact, and all the friends she has now are the same ones she had then, or pretty much, and her husband Leonard is the same, only older, heavier, and the years between high school and now have passed swiftly, in a strong unbroken line. They've been good years, but Sharon can't figure out where in the world they went, or tell much difference between them.

Until she met Raymond, that is. Now she has some high points in her life. But "met" is the wrong word. Until she saw Raymond with "new eyes" is how Sharon thinks of it now.

She went into Stewart's that day in August and showed Raymond her typed recipes and told him what she wanted. He said he thought he could do that. What kind of paper? he wanted to know. What about the cover? Sharon hadn't considered the cover. Raymond Stewart bobbed up and down before her like a jack-in-the-box, asking questions. It made her feel faint, or it might have been the sudden chill of the air-conditioning, she'd just come from standing out in her hot backyard with the hose, watering her garden. "What?" she said. Sharon has a low, pretty voice, and a way of patting her hair. "Sit right down here, honey," Raymond said, "and let me get you a cup of coffee." Which he did, and it was *so strong*, tasting faintly of almonds.

They decided to use pale blue paper, since blue and gold were the school colors. Sharon looked at Raymond Stewart while he snipped and pasted on the coffee table. "Aha!" he shrieked, and "Aha!" Little bits of paper went flying everywhere. Sharon looked around, but nobody seemed to notice: People in Stewart's were used to Raymond. She found herself smiling.

"Hmmm," Raymond said critically, laying out the pages, and "This sounds *yummy*," about Barbara Sutcliff's Strawberries Romanoff. Sharon had never heard a grown man say "yummy" out loud before. She began to pay more attention. That day Raymond was wearing baggy, pleated tan pants—an old man's pants, Sharon thought—a Hawaiian shirt with blue parrots on it, and red rubber flip-flops. "Oh, this sounds *dreadful*," Raymond said as he laid out Louise Dart's famous chicken recipe where you spread drumsticks with apricot preserves and mustard.

"Actually it's pretty good," Sharon said. "*Everybody* makes that." But she was giggling. The strong coffee was making her definitely high, so high that he talked her into naming the cookbook *Home on the Range* (which everybody thought was just darling, as it turned out), and then he drew a cover for it, a woman in a cowboy hat and an apron tending to a whole stovetop full of wildly bubbling pans. The woman had a funny look on her face; puffs of steam came out of some of the pots.

"I used to draw," Sharon said dreamily, watching him.

Raymond has small, white hands with tufts of gold hair on them.

"What did you draw?" He didn't look up.

"Trees," Sharon said. "Pages and pages and pages of trees." As soon as she said it, she remembered it—sitting out on the porch after supper with the pad on her lap, drawing tree after tree with huge flowing branches that reached for God. She didn't tell him the part about God. But suddenly she knew she *could*, if she wanted to. You could say anything to Raymond Stewart, just the way you could say anything to somebody you sat next to on a bus: *anything.*

He grinned at her. His hair stood up in wild blond clumps and behind the thick glasses his magnified eyes were enormous, the pale, flat blue of robins' eggs. "How's that?" He held up the drawing and Sharon said it was fine. Then he signed his name in tiny peaked letters across the bottom of it, like an electrocardiogram, which she didn't expect. Something about him doing this tugged at her heart.

Sharon drank more coffee while he ran off four copies of the recipe booklet; he'd do five hundred more later, if her committee approved. Raymond put these copies into a large flat manila envelope and handed it to her with a flourish and a strange little half-bow. Then somehow, in the midst of standing up and thanking him and taking the envelope—she was all in a flurry—Sharon cut her hand on the flap of the envelope. It was a long, bright cut—a half-moon curve in the soft part of her hand between thumb and index finger. "Oh!" she said.

"Oh my God!" Raymond said dramatically. Together they watched while the blood came up slowly, like little red beads on a string. Then Raymond seized her hand and brought it to his mouth and kissed it!—kissed the cut. When Sharon jerked her hand away, it left a red smear, a bloodstain, on his cheek.

"Oh, I'm sorry! I'm so sorry!" Raymond cried, following Sharon out as she fled through the makeup section of the pharmacy where Missy Harrington was looking at lipstick and that older, redheaded lady was working the cash register, and where nobody, apparently, had noticed *anything*.

"I'll call you about the recipe book," Sharon tossed back over her shoulder. It was only from years of doing everything right that she was able to be so polite . . . or was it? Because what *had* happened, anyway? Nothing, really . . . just not a thing. But Sharon sat in her car for a long time before she started back toward home, not minding how the hot seat burned the backs of her legs. Then, on the way, she tried to remember everything she had ever known about Raymond Stewart.

He was younger—he'd been three or four years behind Sharon in school. Everybody used to call him Highwater because he wore his pants so short that you could always see his little white socks, his little white ankles. He'd been a slight, awkward boy, known for forgetting his books and losing his papers and saying things in class that were totally beside the point. Supposedly, though, he was "bright"; Sharon had had one class with him because he had advanced placement in something, she couldn't remember what now—some kind of English class. How odd that he'd never gone on to college. . . . What Sharon *did* remember, vividly, was Raymond's famous two-year stint as drum major for the high school, after her graduation. Sharon, then a young married woman sitting in the bleachers with her husband, had seen him in this role again and again. Before Leonard Lee was born, Sharon went to all the games with Leonard, who used to be the quarterback.

So she was right there the first time Raymond Stewart— wearing a top hat, white gloves, white boots, and an electric-blue sequined suit which, it was rumored, he had designed himself—came strutting and dancing across the field, leading the band like a professional. Nobody ever saw anything like it! He'd strut, spin, toss his baton so high it seemed lost in the stars, then leap up to catch it and land in a split. Sharon remembered remarking to Leonard once, at a game, that she could hardly connect this Raymond Stewart, the drum major—wheeling like a dervish across the field below them—with that funny little guy who had been, she thought, in her English class. That little guy who wore such high pants. "Well," Leonard had said then, after some deliberation—and Leonard was no dummy—"well, maybe it just took him a while to find the right clothes."

Raymond had a special routine he did while the band played "Blue Suede Shoes" and formed itself into a giant shoe on the field. Everybody in the band had showed more spunk and rhythm then, Sharon thought, than any of them had ever shown before—or since, for that matter. Under Raymond's leadership, the band won two AAA number-one championships, an all-time record for Roxboro High. They even went to play at the Apple Blossom Festival the year the governor's daughter was crowned queen, all because of Raymond Stewart.

And just what had Raymond done since? After his father's suicide, which must have happened around the end of his senior year, he had turned "nervous" for a while. He had gone to work at Stewart's Pharmacy and had continued to live with his mother in their big old nubby green concrete house on Sunset Street. Everybody said something should be done about the house, the shameful way Raymond Stewart had let it run down. Since the leaves had not been raked for years and years, all the grass had died—that carefully tended long sloping lawn which used to be Paul Stewart's pride and joy back in the days when he walked to work every morning in his gleaming white pharmacist's jacket with a flower in his buttonhole, speaking to everybody. Paint was peeling from the dark green shutters now, and some of them hung at crazy angles. The hedge had grown halfway up the windows. The side porch was completely engulfed in wisteria, with vines as thick as your arm. It was just a shame. Of course Raymond Stewart wouldn't notice anything like that, or think about raking leaves . . . and his mother!

Miss Suetta was as crazy as a coot. Raymond hired somebody to stay with her all the time. The Stewarts had plenty of money, of course, but Miss Suetta thought she was dirt poor. She'd sneak off from her companion, and hitchhike to town and go into stores and pick out things, and then cry and say she didn't have any money. So the salespeople would charge whatever it was to Raymond, and then they'd call him to come and get her and drive her home. Sharon had been hearing stories about Miss Suetta Stewart for years and years.

But about Raymond—what else? Every Sunday, he played the organ at the First Methodist Church, in a stirring and dramatic way. The whole choir, including Sharon's Aunt Marge, was completely devoted to him. They all called him Ramón. And he had had his picture in the paper last year for helping to organize the Shady Mountain Players, an amateur theatrical group which so far had put on only one show, about a big rabbit. Sharon saw that, but she couldn't remember if Raymond had had a part in it or not. Mainly you thought of Raymond in connection with weddings—everybody consulted Raymond about wedding plans—or interior decoration. Several of Sharon's friends had hired him, in fact. What he did was help you pick your colors through your astral sign. He didn't *order* anything for you, he just advised. In fact, come to think of it, Sharon herself had ordered some new business cards from Raymond Stewart several years ago, for Leonard when he got his promotion. Gray stock with maroon lettering, which Leonard hadn't liked. Leonard said they looked gay. When he found out where she got them, he said it figured, because Raymond Stewart was probably gay too. Sharon smiled at this memory now, driving home. How funny to find that she knew so much about him, after all! How funny that he'd been right here all along—that you could live in the same town with somebody all these years and just simply never notice them, never think of them once as a person. This idea made Sharon feel so weird she wished she'd never thought it up in the first place.

Then she pulled into her driveway and there was Margaret playing with the hose, pointing it down to drill holes in the soft black dirt of the flower bed. "Stop it! You stop it right now!" Sharon jerked her daughter's little shoulder much harder than she meant to, grabbing the hose.

Later, after Margaret had run in the house yelling and Sharon had turned off the water, she stood out in the heat with the dripping hose and stared, just stared, at the row of little pines that Leonard had planted all along the back of their property, noticing for the first time how much they had grown since he set them out there six years before, when they'd built the house. The pines were big now, as symmetrical as Christmas trees, their green needles glistening in the sun. Sharon thought she might try to draw them. Then she burst into tears, and when Raymond Stewart came by her house in early September to deliver the PTA's five hundred recipe booklets, she went to bed with him.

R aymond was an ardent, imaginative lover. Sometimes he brought her some candy from the pharmacy. Sometimes he brought flowers. Once he brought her a butterfly, still alive, and kissed her on the mouth when she let it go. Sometimes he dressed up for her: He'd wear one of his father's pin-striped suits, or a Panama hat and army-green Bermuda shorts with eight pockets, or a dashiki and sandals, or mechanic's coveralls with "Mike" stitched on the pocket, or jeans and a Jack Daniel's cap. "Honestly!" Sharon would say. Because Raymond thought she was beautiful, she came to *like* her large soft body. She loved the way he made everything seem so special, she loved the way he talked—his high-pitched zany laugh—and how he stroked her tumbling hair. He was endlessly fascinated by how she spent her day, by all the dumb details of her life.

Oh, but there was no time, it seemed, at first, and no place to go—two hours once a week at Sharon's, once Margaret had been deposited at Mother's Morning Out—or late afternoon in the creepy old Stewart house, after the boys came home from school to watch Margaret, while Miss Suetta went to group therapy at the Senior Citizens' Center, with her companion. Miss Suetta hated both group therapy and her companion. Sharon lay giggling in Raymond's four-poster bed on these occasions, aware that if she'd ever acted so silly in her own house, Leonard would have sent her packing years ago. But Raymond gave her scuppernong wine in little green-stemmed crystal glasses. The strong autumn sun came slanting across his bed. The wine was sweet. Raymond was blind as a bat without his glasses. Oh, she could have stayed there forever, covering his whole little face, his whole body with kisses.

Raymond had a way of framing things with words that made them special. He gave events a title. For their affair, he had adopted a kind of wise-guy voice and a way of talking out of the side of his mouth, like somebody in *The Godfather.* "Me and my baby sip *scuppernong wine,*" he'd say—to nobody—rolling his eyes. Or, "Me and my baby *take in a show,*" when once they actually did this, the following summer when Sharon's kids spent the night with her mother and Leonard went to the National Guard. Raymond picked an arty movie for them to see, named *The Night of the Shooting Stars,* and they drove over to Greenville together to see it after meeting in a 7-Eleven at the city limits, where Sharon left her car. *The Night of the Shooting Stars* turned out to be very weird in Sharon's opinion and not anything you would really want to make a movie about. But Raymond thought it was great. Later, on the way back, he drove down a dirt road off the highway and parked in the warm rustling woods.

"Me and my baby *make out!*" Raymond crowed, pulling her into his arms. Oh, it was crazy!

And it got worse. They grew greedier and greedier.

Several times, Raymond had just left by the back door when Leonard came in at the front. Several times, going or coming, Sharon encountered Raymond's mother, who never seemed to notice until the day Sharon picked her up hitchhiking downtown and drove her back to the house on Sunset Street. Just before Miss Suetta went in the front door, she stopped dead in her tracks and turned to point a long skinny finger back at Sharon. "Just who *is* this woman?" she asked loudly. And then her companion came and thanked Sharon and guided Miss Suetta inside.

By this time, of course, Sharon called him Ramón.

After two years, he finally talked her into going to a motel, the new Ramada Inn in Greenville. Built on a grander scale than anything else in the county, this Ramada Inn was really more like a hotel, he told her, promising saunas and a sunken bar and an indoor pool and Nautilus equipment. "You know I wouldn't do any of that," said Sharon. Leonard had to go out of town on a selling trip anyway—Leonard can sell or trade anything, which is what he does for the coal company he works for. For instance, he will trade a piece of land for a warehouse, or a rear-end loader for a computer. Sharon doesn't know exactly what Leonard does. But he was out of town, so she let Alister and Leonard Lee spend the night with their friends and asked her mother to keep Margaret. "Why?" her mother had asked. "Well, I've been spotting between my periods," Sharon said smoothly, "and Dr. King wants me to go over to Greenville for some tests." She could lie like a rug! But before Sharon saw Raymond with new eyes, she had never lied in her whole life. Sharon felt wonderful and terrible, checking into the Ramada Inn with Raymond as Mr. and Mrs. John Deere. The clerk didn't bat an eye.

This Ramada was as fancy, as imposing as advertised. Their room was actually a suite, with a color TV and the promised sunken tub, and a king-size bed under a tufted velvet spread and a big brass lamp as large as Margaret. Sharon stifled a sob. She was feeling edgy and kind of blue. It was one thing to find an hour here and an hour there, but another thing to do this. "All I want for Christmas is to sleep with you *all night long*," Raymond had said. Sharon wanted this too. But she hadn't thought it would be so hard. She looked around the room. "How much did this cost?" she asked. "Oh, not much. Anyway, I've got plenty of *money*," Raymond said airily, and Sharon stared at him. This was true, but she always forgot it.

Raymond went out for ice and came back and made two big blue drinks out of rum and a bottled mix. The drinks looked like Windex. "Me and my baby go Hawaiian," Raymond said gravely, clicking his glass against hers. Then they got drunk and had a wonderful time. The next morning Sharon was terrified of seeing somebody she knew, but it turned out that nobody at all was around. Nobody. Raymond joked about this as they walked down the long pale corridor. He made his voice into a Rod Serling *Twilight*

Zone voice. "They think they're checking out of . . . the *ghost motel*," he said.

Then Sharon imagined that they had really died in a wreck on the way to the motel, only they didn't know it. When they turned a corner and saw themselves reflected in a mirror in the lobby, she screamed.

"She screams, but no one can hear her in . . . the *ghost motel*," said Raymond. He carried his clothes in a laundry bag.

"No, hush, I mean it," Sharon said.

She looked in the mirror while Raymond paid the bill, and it seemed to her then that she was wavy and insubstantial, and that Raymond, when he came up behind her, was nothing but air. They held hands tightly and didn't talk, all the way back to the 7-Eleven where Sharon had parked her car.

And now, Raymond is all excited about the eclipse. He's been talking about it for weeks. He's just like a kid. Sharon's real kids, Leonard Lee and Alister and Margaret, have been studying eclipses at school, but they couldn't care less.

"I want to be with you, baby, to view the eclipse." Raymond has said this to Sharon again and again. He has made them both little contraptions out of cardboard, with peepholes, so they won't burn their retinas. Luckily, the eclipse is set for one-thirty on a Tuesday afternoon, so the children are at school. Leonard is at work.

Raymond arrives promptly at one, dressed in his father's white pharmacist's jacket. "I thought I ought to look scientific," he says, twirling around in Sharon's kitchen to give her the full effect. His high giggle ricochets off the kitchen cabinets. He has brought a bottle of pink champagne. He pops the cork with a flourish and offers her a glass. Which Sharon accepts gladly because in truth she's not feeling so good—it's funny how that lie she told her mother a couple of months ago seems to be coming true. Probably her uterus is just falling apart. The truth is, she's getting *old*—sometimes she feels just ancient, a hundred years older than Raymond.

Sharon sips the champagne slowly while Raymond opens all of her kitchen cabinets and pokes around inside them.

"What are you looking for?" she finally asks.

"Why—nothing!" When Raymond smiles, his face breaks into crinkles all over. He clasps her forcefully. "I like to see where you keep things," he says. "You're an endless mystery to me, baby." He kisses her, then pulls out a pocket watch she's never seen before. Perhaps he bought it just for the eclipse. "One-twelve," he says. "Come on, you *heavenly body* you. It's time to go outside."

In spite of herself, Sharon has gotten excited too. They take plastic lawn chairs and sit down right in the middle of the backyard, near the basketball goal but well away from the pines, where they can get the most open view. It's a cloudless day in early March. Sharon's daffodils are blooming. She has thought this all through ahead of time: The only neighbor with a view of her backyard, Mrs. Hodges, is gone all day. Raymond refills his glass with champagne. Sharon's lettuce is coming up, she notices, in crinkly green waves at the end of the garden. But Raymond is telling her what will happen next, lecturing her in a deep scientific voice which makes him sound exactly like the guy on *Wild Kingdom*: "When the moon passes directly between the earth and the sun so that its shadow falls upon the earth, there's a solar eclipse, visible from the part of the earth's surface on which the shadow lies. So it's the shadow of the moon which will pass across us."

I don't care! Sharon nearly screams it. *All I want*, she thinks, *honey, all I ever want is you.* Raymond sits stiffly upright in her plastic lawn chair, his head leaning to the side in a practiced, casual manner, lecturing about the umbra and penumbra. He has smoothed his spiky blond hair down for this occasion and it gleams in the early spring sun.

"A total solar eclipse occurs only once in every four hundred years in any one place. Actually this won't be a total eclipse, not where we are. If we'd driven over to Greensboro, we would have been right in the center of it." For a minute, his face falls. "Maybe we should have done that."

"Oh, no," Sharon assures him. "I think this is just fine." She sips her champagne while Raymond shows her how to look through the little box in order to see the eclipse. Raymond consults his watch—one-fifteen. Mrs. Hodges's golden retriever, Ralph, starts barking.

"Dogs will bark," Raymond intones. "Animals will go to bed. Pregnant women will have their babies. Birds will cease to twitter."

"*Twitter?*" Sharon says. "Well, they sure are twittering now." Sharon has a lot of birds because of the bird feeder Alister made in Shop II.

"*Trust me.* It's coming," says Raymond.

While Sharon and Raymond sit in her backyard with their boxes on their knees, waiting, Sharon has a sudden awful view of them from somewhere else, a view of how they must look, doing this, drinking champagne. It's so wild! Ralph barks and the birds twitter, and then, just as Raymond promised, they cease. Ralph ceases too. Raymond squeezes Sharon's hand. A hush falls, a shadow falls, the very air seems to thicken suddenly, to darken around them, but still it's not *dark*. It's the weirdest thing Sharon has ever seen. It's like it's getting colder too, all of a sudden. She bets the temperature has dropped at least ten degrees. "Oh, baby! Oh, honey!" Raymond says. Through the peephole in her cardboard box, Sharon sees the moon, a dark object moving across the sun's face and shutting more and more of its bright surface from view, and then it's really twilight.

"Me and my baby view the eclipse," says Raymond.

Sharon starts crying.

The sun is nothing now but a crazy shining crescent, a ghost sun. Funny shadows run all over everything—all over Sharon's garden, her house, her pine trees, the basketball goal, all over Raymond. His white jacket seems alive, dimly rippling. Sharon feels exactly like somebody big is walking on her grave. Then the shadows are gone, and it's nearly dark. Sharon can see stars. Raymond kisses her, and then the eclipse is over.

"It was just like they said it would be!" he says. "Just exactly!" He's very excited. Then they go to bed, and when Margaret comes home from school he's still there, in the hall bathroom.

"Hi, honey," says Sharon, who ran quickly into the kitchen when she first heard Margaret, so as to appear busy. Sharon moves things around in the refrigerator.

"Who's *that*?" Margaret drops her knapsack and points straight at Raymond, who has chosen just this moment to come out of the bathroom waving Sharon's new Dustbuster. Margaret is a skinny, freckled little girl who's mostly serious. Now she's in first grade.

"What's *this*?" Raymond waves the Dustbuster. He's delighted by gadgets, but whenever he buys one, it breaks.

"I'll show you," Margaret says. She demonstrates the Dustbuster while Raymond buttons his daddy's white pharmacy jacket.

"See?" Margaret says gravely.

"That's *amazing*," Raymond says.

Sharon, watching them, thinks she will die. But Raymond leaves before the boys get home, and Margaret doesn't mention him until the next afternoon. "He was nice," Margaret says them.

"Who, honey?" Sharon is frying chicken.

"That man who was here. Who was he?" Margaret asks again.

"Oh, just nobody," Sharon says. Because it's true. Her affair with Raymond Stewart is over now as suddenly and as mysteriously as it began. Sharon aches with loss. When she tells Raymond, he'll be upset, as she is upset, but he'll live, as she will. He'll find things to do. He has just been given the part of Ben in the Shady Mountain Players production of *The Glass Menagerie*, for instance, a part he's always wanted. He'll be okay. Sharon plans to say, "Raymond, I will never love anyone in the world as much as I love you." This is absolutely true. She loves him, she will love him forever with a fierce sweet love that will never die. For Raymond Stewart will never change. He'll grow older, more eccentric. People will point him out. Although their mothers will tell them not to, children will follow him in the street, begging him to talk funny and make faces. Maybe he'll have girlfriends. But nobody will ever love him as much as Sharon—he's shown her things. She knows this. And oh, she'll be around, she'll run into

Raymond from time to time—choosing Leonard's new business cards, for instance, when Leonard gets another promotion, or making up the Art Guild flier, or—years and years from now—ordering Margaret's wedding invitations.

About the Author

Lee Smith is the author of fifteen works of fiction, including *Oral History, Fair and Tender Ladies,* and *Mrs. Darcy and the Blue-Eyed Stranger.* She has received many awards, including the North Carolina Award for Literature—and an Academy Award in Literature from the American Academy of Arts and Letters; her novel *The Last Girls* was a *New York Times* bestseller as well as winner of the Southern Book Critics Circle Award. She lives in North Carolina.